Hidden Secrets

"Secrets and Second Chances," Book 2

Hidden Secrets

Donna M. Zadunajsky

Copyright

ISBN: 978-1523225088 – (13) - Print copy
ISBN: 1523225084 – (10) – Print copy
ISBN: 978-1523225132 (13) – Large Print
ISBN: 1523225130 (10) – Large Print
ISBN: 978-1-938037-55-9 – Ingram Print
ISBN: 978-1-938037-56-6 – Ingram eBook

This novel is a work of fiction.

Names, characters, places and incidents are either the product of the author's imagination or are used fictitiously. Any resemblance to actual persons, living or dead, events, or places is entirely confidential.

Part I

"*Love is that condition in which the happiness of another person is essential to your own.*"

Robert A. Heinlein

What we think is more important in life, is just an excuse for not trying hard enough for what is right in front of us...

Donna M. Zadunajsky

Prelude:

What would you do if you found a book, a journal hidden away, filled with secrets—things you weren't meant to know; things you should've known from the beginning?

So the question remains, how well does anyone really know his or her own spouse, sister, brother, mother, or father?

You could be living under the same roof for five, ten, even twenty years, and not **_really_** know one another. Even before they became your significant other, did their parents or siblings know them better than anyone else did? *Did your family keep things hidden?*

Siblings don't always share their secrets with each other. They are not close. They most likely won't get along with one another until they become adults, and still maybe even then, not see eye to eye!

What if you're an only child, no one with which to share anything? *What if* one day you're all alone? Your parents or spouse dies, goes to heaven, and you one-day stumble across a secret that your so-called loved ones have been hiding from you. What would you do? Of course, you would read it. You wouldn't be able to help yourself. You would be too curious the moment you opened the book and read the first line. Especially, if you saw your name written as one of the words.

What if everything you thought you knew about *your family, your spouse, your lover* were all lies? Something they thought was better kept hidden from the one person they supposedly loved the most.

Even then, no one really knows anyone, do they?

Chapter 1

I opened the rear door of my grey Infiniti Sedan and grabbed my briefcase. I decided this morning I'd have my second graders work on an art project about what they did over their long weekend. I, on the other hand, had spent most of my time on the sofa with my feet elevated.

I was nearly six months pregnant and feeling the fatigue in my legs and feet. My job as a schoolteacher had me standing for long periods at a time. I knew I'd eventually have to start teaching my pupils from my chair, as much as possible.

A strong breeze ruffled my light brown shoulder-length hair. I brushed the hair away from my eyes, tucking several strands behind my ear. I closed the rear car door and made my way inside the school.

Every morning, I'd stop at the front office to gather papers from my mailbox and chat with my friend, Veronica Rowan.

Veronica was a secretary in the front office. She answered the phones and assisted anyone that came into the office needing help or advice about school-related issues. She also helped with daily tasks, when needed.

When my husband Tim and I moved from Florida to Illinois after college, I didn't know anyone in town. The first time I had met Veronica was when I started teaching at Haven Elementary—ten years ago.

I considered Veronica a good friend. Not a best friend, like my two friends Alexis and Ashley, but still a friend no less. I am a person with trust issues, dating back to my teens. Once I made the choice of trusting you and accepting you into my life, you became someone dear to me. The worst mistake anyone could make was to betray that trust, break that bond! A cheating boyfriend with your best friend would do that to you. As I got older, I knew who my friends really were. Too many times, I was burned and left to pick up the pieces.

Once a month, Veronica and I would accompany each other to the library for our mystery book club. On occasion, we'd get together for dinner at my house or sometimes, Veronica's. Veronica's boyfriend Pat Atkins, who worked with Tim at a law firm they both leased and shared, would play pool downstairs in the man cave, while the two of us sat and talked about the latest fashion, school, and the next book we were going to read.

"Good morning, Carla," Veronica sang.

"Good morning," I replied, smiling back at her.

"Oh!" Veronica shrieked. "I love your dress. It's perfect for the weather we've been having." Her blue eyes sparkled in the fluorescent light.

"Thank you. I've been wanting to wear it before I got too big." This morning I had chosen a maternity dress with a floral design that flowed past my knees. I usually wore maternity pants, but with the temperatures reaching the mid-seventies to eighties these past few days in February, of all months, I wanted to stay as comfortable as possible.

"Yes. A little too warm for this time of year, but I won't complain," I expressed. *Even though I was from Ohio, I honestly missed living in Florida where the days are always warm;* the thought lingered in my mind.

The phone rang before Veronica could reply. She raised her pointer finger to me, indicating to give her a minute. As Veronica talked on the phone, I whispered that I'd see her later and waved goodbye. Veronica nodded and continued her conversation on the phone, while twisting her finger in a lock of sandy blonde hair, resting on her shoulder.

I left the office and walked down the hall towards my classroom. My eyes sketched over the drawings that were hung on the wall between each classroom. The pictures taped to the wall told me what was taught in that specific class. The science room, where the third graders were taught, had poster boards with different types of weather on them.

Social Studies, also done by third graders, had photos of every president that had served in the United States, and on the other side of the door hung the Declaration of Independence.

When I came to the next room, I stopped and admired the drawings on the wall. My second graders drew the pictures. I couldn't get over how imaginative they were at such a young age. Their dreams expressed and painted on paper.

For a moment, my thoughts went to my unborn child. Him or her, what would they grow up to be? There were many possibilities, of course. Every day that I'd spent teaching the next generation gave my life meaning. I smiled, unlocked the door to the room, and flipped on the lights.

Before leaving for the long weekend, I'd written, *"Good morning second graders,"* on the blackboard. I always thought of my students as my own and wanted them to feel comfortable and not overwhelmed in my class.

I made my way to the desk in front of me and opened the bottom drawer. Taking the straps of my purse off my shoulder, I set the bag inside and closed it. I laid my briefcase on the desk and pushed the buttons, until I heard a *click.* I took out the graded papers I did over the weekend and closed the lid, setting the case under the desk.

Within a few minutes, all of the students would arrive at school. I walked to the back of the room, grabbed a handful of colored drawing paper, and started placing one sheet on each desk.

The desks were placed four in a group so the children could interact with one another. Each desk had the student's name written on colored paper and taped neatly at the top. When I finished, I stood at the chalkboard, writing five new words for my students to learn.

The room was quiet, except for the *clacking* of the chalk hitting the chalkboard. My mind focused only on what I was doing and nothing else. At peace with myself before my students were to arrive and fill the empty room.

I was so engrossed in my work that I didn't hear or see the little girl standing in the doorway. I jumped, my heart pounding beneath my dress, when I heard the young voice speak to me.

"Good morning, Mrs. Michaels," the little girl greeted.

I quickly turned, grabbing the ledge of the blackboard. Once I saw who it was, I smiled and exhaled the breath I was holding. Ever since my pregnancy, I'd become easier to scare. Something I'd have to get accustomed to.

"Good morning to you too, Samantha. How was your weekend?"

The smile on Samantha's face turned to a frown from what I'd asked. Samantha with her wavy dirty-blonde hair, shrugged her shoulders, and without saying another word, turned and walked to the back of the room. She placed her paper bag lunch in a bin at the back of the class and took her seat.

I wasn't surprised that Samantha was the first to arrive. In fact, I'd be more concerned if she weren't here.

I watched as Samantha took her seat, looked at her hands, and then a single tear slid down her face. This wasn't the first time I'd seen her cry, but I wished it was the last. Something inside me told me things were not going well at home. I'd noticed bruises on her arms and legs. When I had asked Samantha what had happened, she had replied that she fell off her bike or tripped over her toys that she'd left in the middle of the floor.

Of course, I thought for sure Samantha was lying to me. That she didn't want me as her teacher to know what really happened to her. I felt certain that Samantha was being abused. When I confronted Principal Steve Clapton, he said he'd look into the situation and get back to me, but that had been weeks ago.

I walked up behind Samantha and combed my fingers gently over the girl's soft waves. I placed a tissue in Samantha's hand, and then whispered in her ear that everything would be all right and that I was here, if she needed someone to talk to. Samantha smiled, wiped the tears from her face and shoved the Kleenex in the pocket of her shorts.

Throughout the day as I taught my students, I kept my eye on Samantha. I wished with all my heart I could protect her from whomever was hurting her.

A thought came to me while I was at lunch. I'd send a note home with Samantha, requesting that her parents meet with me. I would start with how well Samantha was doing in my class, and then *finesse* in some questions about the bruises I'd noticed. If their story matched Samantha's, then I'd *try* to believe that they weren't abusing her.

~ ~ ~ ~ ~

The bell rang and I quickly glanced up at the clock. I couldn't believe how fast the day had flown by. It felt like the students had just arrived, and now they were going home for the day.

Mrs. Larson from across the hall came over and gathered up the students. I was relieved it was Mrs. Larson's day to take the kids to the buses. I was feeling extremely tired and was looking forward to putting my feet up when I got home.

Before the children left, I handed Samantha an envelope and requested that she give it to her parents when she arrived home from school. Samantha's face clouded over with fear, but I reassured her that it was nothing to worry about. That I just wanted to meet with her mom and dad, and inform them of Samantha's accomplishments and how proud I was of her and her artwork. Samantha then smiled and hurried out of the room with the other children to catch their bus.

After collecting the drawings from each desk, I made my way towards the front of the classroom. This morning I'd thought I felt a *twinge*, maybe a little pain. *But,* I had stopped worrying or at least I'd tried. I didn't want to be one of those emotional pregnant women, filled with uneasiness. Even though I had reason to worry, this being my fifth pregnancy and the only one I'd carried this far into term.

Before I could reach the desk, I grabbed my belly as pain shot up through my mid-section, feeling like I'd been stabbed with a knife. Not that I'd ever been stabbed before, but this had to be the sensation.

My knees buckled from under me and I fell to the floor. Kneeling on all fours, I lifted my right hand to my belly. Warmth rolled down the length of my inner thigh. Using the hand that held my bulging belly, I maneuvered my body just enough to lift the floral print maternity dress and reached a hand underneath. When I brought my hand back in front of me, I saw red blood covering my fair skin.

My thoughts hazed over and returned to the children I taught. Class had ended and my students had left, just mere minutes ago. Second graders with all the other tragedies they would witness as they aged, shouldn't have to see their teacher like this.

"No!" I gasped, as shooting pain spiraled through me. "This can't be happening! Not now, not again!"

~ ~ ~ ~ ~

As my mind desperately fought against what I knew my body was doing—trying to reject my baby—I couldn't help but remember all I had been through. It flashed through my thoughts in quick, jagged scenes that showed the heartbreak I had been through that I was so sure this was a thing of the past. *Was the past coming back to haunt me again?*

Dr. Shaffer, my OB/GYN, had told me that everything was moving along as planned. I wasn't having any morning sickness or complications. I was told the baby was fine, that everything *seemed* fine. My past pregnancies, I'd never made it to the second trimester.

When I asked about being tested, the doctor had first told me that since it was my first miscarriage, he couldn't test me unless I continued to have them. The doctor assured me that many women had miscarriages; it was just the body's way of rejecting the fetus, if there was something wrong with the fetus or the pregnancy. The doctor explained that sometimes a healthy embryo could be rejected if it had adhered to an area in the womb, which wouldn't allow the fetus to develop correctly.

"This doesn't happen often," Dr. Shaffer had explained, "and usually it's only with a first pregnancy. If you continue to miscarry then we will run tests to determine if there is something wrong with your embryotic eggs or the health of the womb itself."

After the second miscarriage, the doctor ran a few tests, but every time he'd found nothing wrong. As time went by, I started having abdominal pain. Sometimes the pain was so intense, I had to crawl on my hands and knees to get from one room to the other. That's when the doctor requested a laparoscopy to be performed.

After the surgery, the doctor informed me and my husband that I had Endometriosis and scar tissue throughout my abdominal area. He concluded that he removed all of the Endometriosis and scar tissue, and that I should be fine now and would be able to get pregnant without any more complications. Three-months later, I got pregnant, but lost that baby as well. Eight years of trying and five pregnancies later, I'd made it to my sixth month, almost to the third trimester.

Holding one hand on my belly, I inched my way to the front of the classroom. I reached for the corner of the desk and pulled myself up. The school phone lay just out of my reach.

I slowly made my way around the left side of the desk and slid my hand across the top towards the phone, while the right hand hugged the life inside me. Shooting pains came and went, but I could feel that the blood continued to seep.

A sharp cramp caused me to knock the phone out of its cradle as I screamed out in pain. I didn't know if I had time to call my husband Tim and tell him what was happening. I knew I needed to get to the hospital, now—before it was too late. I pressed the speaker button and dialed the front office, waiting for Veronica to answer.

"Hey, I was just about to call you and see if you wanted to go to the bookstore with me," Veronica said, her voice high and perky.

"Veronica, I need help," I cried out. "Something's wrong with the baby!"

"Oh, my God! Are you going into labor? Oh, my God, oh, my God," Veronica kept shouting into the phone.

"I don't know. There's so much blood. Hurry, please!" I shouted.

Another contraction ripped through my abdomen, making me scream out in pain. My legs went weak and I took a step forward. My right foot caught the edge of the briefcase sticking out from under the desk. I went down, my head *whacked* the corner of the desk, and I fell to the floor. All went black...

Chapter 2

I opened my eyes and breathed in the cool stale air around me. My throat was parched and my mouth tasted of cotton. At first, I wasn't sure where I was, but the smell of antiseptic entering my nostrils quickly defused the uncertainty.

I placed my hand gently on the right side of my head that ached. I sucked in a quick breath from the touch and tried to remember what had happened to me. My mind drew a blank. I didn't even know what day it was. How long I'd been in the hospital.

When my eyes adjusted to the light, I saw my husband sitting hunched over in a chair next to the bed, his face resting in his hands.

His short brown hair looked unruly; as he lifted his head and glanced over at me, a small smile surfaced. The wetness in his blue eyes glistened in the light. I wasn't sure if he'd been crying, though the redness in his eyes told me he had.

He moved towards me and kissed my lips, then gently grazed his finger across my forehead, brushing the hair away.

"You're finally awake?" he whispered. "How are you feeling?"

"Okay, I guess. A little thirsty," I grumbled, and then swallowed as I tried to moisten my dry throat. "How long have I been in the hospital?"

"One night. You were brought in yesterday afternoon, and have been unconscious until just now," he replied.

I watched as he stood and walked to a table on the other side of the room and poured a glass of water. I pushed a button on the side of the bed, making it rise. Tim helped me sit up and then handed me the plastic cup. After taking several big gulps, I handed the glass back to him half empty.

It was then that I noticed how flat the blankets lay upon me. I reached my hand to my belly and quickly turned my head towards Tim.

I watched as his lips parted, but he said nothing. Part of me didn't want to ask, to know that I'd lost yet another baby. We stared at each other, neither one saying a word. It wasn't like we hadn't been here before, but not knowing made me feel…uneasy.

"I'm sorry," I whimpered like a sad puppy, feeling like my world was falling apart around me, again.

"Sorry for what?" Tim questioned, as he sat back in the chair.

"For not being able to give you a child." Tears filled my eyes, and then slid down my cheeks. My husband looked shocked somehow by what I'd said. More of a, *"What are you talking about?"* look.

Tim inhaled deeply. "She's in NICU, Neonatal Intensive Care Unit," he replied, watching as a puzzled look appeared on my face.

"The…the baby's alive?" The words stuck in my throat before registering in my mind. This was wonderful news!

"Yes, we have a daughter," he replied, giving me a somewhat forced smile.

"A daughter? Have you seen her?" My heart quickened, filling my body with excitement.

"Yes. One of the nurses that came in to check on you asked if I'd seen our baby. When I replied, *I hadn't,* she took me to see her."

"We have a baby girl. She's…she's alive?" I breathed, still in shock that the baby had survived at all.

Everything that had happened came flooding back. The pain, the blood—I was certain when I saw all that blood that I'd lost the baby. *But* I hadn't. This time the baby survived and was down the hall waiting for her mother to come and hold her. I was finally a *Mom.* My face lit up and I couldn't stop myself from smiling. I wanted to jump out of bed and run to her.

"Yes, she's…." he paused. "She's beautiful just like her mother and has your brown hair," Tim finally said.

I wasn't thinking about the occasional pulsating pain I was experiencing. I just wanted to see my baby girl. My daughter was alive and that's all that mattered to me. *Yet,* I could sense there was something Tim wasn't telling me, but wasn't quite sure what it was. I thought I knew my husband well, but there were times I couldn't read his face. He'd close himself off from the world, and I'd have to wait until he was ready to talk to me. I thought he'd be thrilled that this baby survived, but a part of me started to wonder if there was something more, something I didn't know about—yet.

A tall slim nurse came strolling into the room. I observed as Tim stood, making his way to the window so the nurse could do her job, and he wouldn't be in her way.

"Oh, good! You're awake. I was wondering when you'd open your eyes," the nurse chirped, then flaunted a smile.

"She just woke up a few minutes ago," Tim reported from across the room.

The nurse kept her eyes on me as she took my vitals and wrote them down, "So, have you decided on a name for your baby yet?"

"Yes, Tim and I want to name her Mya Ann," I replied with giddiness in my voice.

"That's such a beautiful name. What made you want to name her Mya Ann?" the nurse asked.

"Because she's my miracle baby," I expressed.

The nurse smiled, "That's so lovely, dear." She patted my hand, then without another word, left the room.

I called to Tim, who seemed to be in another world. "Tim, are you there?" I asked again.

"What? Yeah. Sorry, I didn't hear you calling me," he replied, making his way to the chair and sitting back down.

"The nurse said she'll take me to see our daughter in a few minutes."

Tim smiled, holding my hand in his. "Oh, well…"

"Are you okay? Is there something wrong?" I questioned.

He swallowed, "Not wrong, but there's something I should tell you before you see the baby."

"Okay, what is it?" I searched his face, looking for an answer, but not finding one.

"I want you to be prepared when you see her. She's…"

"She's what?" I whispered, feeling more scared as the seconds ticked by.

"Our baby is in a special open warmer hooked to machines. She's extremely small, and you won't be able to hold her, yet."

I said nothing in return. What was there to say? I had been in this same predicament numerous times before. *But,* this time the baby had survived. *At least for now*, I quickly forced the negativity away. My eyes moved from Tim's face to his chest, and then I turned my head and stared at the wall in front of me.

Tears slid down my face as grief sunk in. I didn't want to know any more than what he'd already told me. I didn't want to lose this baby, not like the others. I knew I needed to stay positive and not think about Mya dying, but the tears wouldn't stop pouring from my eyes.

Chapter
3

An hour later, the same nurse from earlier came back in the room. "Are you ready to go see your daughter?"

I nodded and waited anxiously for the nurse to help me sit up and get into a wheelchair. The slower I moved, the less pain I caused myself.

Once inside the NICU, I glanced through a large glass window.

The nurse, who had brought me, knelt down beside the wheelchair. "Can you see your daughter?" the tall slim nurse asked.

I nodded, again. It was as if I was at a loss for words. I was seeing Mya for the first time. My eyes filled up with tears once more as I looked at my tiny baby hooked to multiple wires and tubes. I wanted to hold her so badly, but the nurse had told me I couldn't go inside just yet.

The nurse squeezed my hand, "It's overwhelming, I know. But you have to understand that your baby was born way too early and has a lot of growing to do."

I sat quiet, and then said, "Tell me what's wrong with her."

The nurse looked at Mya, and then back at me, gazing into my eyes, "Your daughter's lungs are immature and need respiratory support. Babies at this age also require a ventilator until the lungs can mature enough for them to breathe on their own," the nurse said, and then looked through the glass window before continuing. "She's also being fed through a UVC line, which is an IV line through the umbilical vein. Her ability to suck and swallow has not matured enough to feed orally," the nurse swallowed. "Infections can also be a huge problem, but we are monitoring her every second and have machines telling us what is going on. She's in good hands, but…but there are other things that can go wrong. Just don't give up on her; she's a fighter, I can tell," the nurse squeezed my hand one more time before looking away.

I could only nod as the tears continued to roll down my face. If nothing else, I had to have faith that this baby would survive.

~ ~ ~ ~ ~

Back in my room, there was still no Tim. He'd left earlier after telling me about the baby and hadn't returned. Part of me was worried about him, but also knew that work played a part in his moods sometimes.

I reached for the phone on the nightstand and dialed a number. I needed someone other than my husband to talk to, but ended up leaving a voicemail as my friend Alexis Finley who lived in Florida hadn't answered the phone. I decided to give my other friend Ashley who lived in Ohio a call as well.

Ten minutes later, after I finished talking to my friend Ashley, I could feel there was something going on with her, but hadn't wanted to pry. There was an unfamiliar strangeness in my friend's voice, something she wasn't telling me. On the other hand, maybe things were fine, and I just thought the worst. I didn't want or need to start worrying about something I had no idea about. Besides, Ashley was in Ohio and I was here in Illinois.

I had nothing else to do but listen to everything going on around me. The intercom howled out codes and carts with their squeaky wheels were pushed down the hall outside my room. No one came in to check on me. It was just me and my mind, which wasn't always a bad thing, at least not right now. Not since I was released last year from therapy. All I could think about was my baby and how tiny she looked.

I wasn't in the mood to watch television so I just glanced around the room, my eyes looking at nothing in particular.

I wasn't sure how much time had passed when the phone next to me started to ring. I reached over and grabbed the phone.

"Hello?"

"Carla?" the woman's voice on the other end asked.

"Yes, this is Carla. May I ask who's calling?"

"It's Alexis, Alexis Finley," my friend replied.

"Alexis, oh, my God! It's so nice to hear from you. I take it you got my message?"

"Yes, yes I did. Is everything okay?"

"I'm fine, now," I replied.

"What's wrong? Why are you in the hospital?"

"Well, it's a long story, but to get you up to speed since… what, seven months ago?"

"Yeah, sorry it's been so long."

"Well, I was pregnant and had a daughter."

"I didn't know you were pregnant. You didn't say anything at the funeral," Alexis questioned.

"That's because I wasn't pregnant yet."

"What do you mean? It's only been seven months, not nine."

"I was early. I was only six months pregnant when I went into labor, if you want to call it that."

"Oh, dear. How is the baby doing?"

"She's in NICU, right now. They're doing everything they can for her. All we can do is pray she'll survive and get stronger." Tears poured from my eyes as I spoke to my best friend.

Silence filled the line between us. I thought we had been disconnected as I let a few seconds pass between us. My friend Alexis Finley worked for NASA, and I knew she'd been busy with work and hadn't made the time to call and see how I was doing. And now...now I had to tell Alexis I had a premature baby and didn't know if she would survive. My friend had enough sadness in her life to worry about. Seven months ago Alexis's husband Jay, Tim's best friend, had committed suicide, which was the last time we had spoken.

"Are you still there?" I asked.

"Yes, sorry. I just...I don't know what to say."

"You know I call you every few weeks, even if you don't return my calls," I reminded.

"I know and I'm sorry for that. I have no excuse for not calling you back. It surprises me that you still call," Alexis replied.

"Are you kidding? You're my best friend and I know you work all the time, but you'll always be my friend no matter what happens. Besides, I knew you were going through a tough time when Jay died and all, but I figured once time passed you'd reach out to me," I said.

"Carla, I'm so sorry about not being a good friend to you."

"You are a good friend. What would make you say that? Look, it's not important. What matters now is that you called me back, and we're talking?"

"Yes. I guess, you're right."

"Yeah, I am." We both laughed. "So, when do you think you can take off work and come for a visit?" I asked, knowing she'd give me some kind of excuse why she couldn't come.

The phone went quiet before my friend responded. "I have to go through my schedule first and see what I can do," Alexis quickly added.

"Okay, I guess. I do hope you can make time to see me. I mean us," I replied, hoping my friend would make the trip up to see me.

"I promise to come visit you soon. I just have a few things going on at the moment."

"I'll hold you to that promise."

"I know you will. Well, I better go; I have some things to take care of, and I'll call you soon," Alexis concluded.

"Sounds good. Alexis?"

"Yes."

"Is everything okay with you? You sound like there's something wrong. Something you're not telling me."

"I'm fine, really I am. No need to worry about me. Look, I'll call you soon okay? We'll talk then."

"Sure, I'll talk to you soon." Before I could get the last word out, I heard a *click*.

I held the phone out in front of me, my face looking bewildered. *Had I caught my friend Alexis at a bad time? Or, did Alexis not want to talk to me? Though, she had been the one that called me.* The questions rolled around in my head. I wasn't sure, but decided I'd wait a week or two and call my friend back. Maybe then I could find out what was wrong with Alexis.

My mind wandered back to the first time we'd met in college. I was sitting by myself as I usually did in the library when Alexis walked up to me and asked if she could sit at the table. After a few awkward moments, we started chatting and became friends.

I had told Alexis that I'd moved from Ohio to Florida after I graduated high school to attend the University of Tallahassee. Of course, finding that odd, Alexis had asked why I moved down here when they had great schools up north. I had replied, "The warmer weather, of course." We both had laughed at my response and began an inseparable friendship.

In college, we'd hung out every day after classes and did many things together; even though we were in different classes, we met up at the library and worked on our homework together. After I met Tim, who had become my husband, we continued to hang out. Tim had introduced Alexis to his best friend, Jay Finley. Tim and Jay were both studying to be lawyers, except Jay changed classes and decided to take business and accounting, a year later.

Alexis and Jay got married right after college and started a family, moving to the Cape Canaveral area. Eventually, Alexis got her dream job working at NASA.

$$\sim \sim \sim \sim \sim$$

Tim entered the room just as I put the phone back in its cradle and sat down next to me. I took my hand off the phone and turned towards him. I could tell there was something on his mind, but before I could ask, he spoke.

"Hey, how are you feeling?"

"I'm doing better, not as much pain as earlier."

He reached and pulled my hand to his lips, giving me a gentle kiss. "You know I love you more than life itself, right? And that I would do anything to make sure you're happy?" His eyes focused on mine.

"Yes, I know. You've told me this before. Tim, what's this all about? Why are you acting so strange?" I knew by the sound of his voice and the jitter of his leg that there was something wrong, something he needed to talk to me about.

"There's something I need to tell you before the doctor comes in to see you."

My heart began to speed up from the words he'd just said. *Had something happened to our baby after I'd last seen her? Oh, God, please not my Mya!* I screamed inside my head. I quickly swallowed the bile now rising in my throat, and asked, "What…what is it that you need to talk to me about?" *I didn't know if I could go through this again,* I thought as I watched him take a long deep breath in, filling up his lungs, and then exhaling.

"When I got to the hospital after I received the call about what had happened to you, I met with the doctor who was on call that delivered our baby. Dr. Brooks said…" Tim paused.

I felt a little relieved that Tim had mentioned yesterday and not the present time. "What did he say?" My eyes searched his face for any kind of answer.

"Carla, he had…" The door to the room swooshed opened and a man wearing a white doctor's coat came strolling in.

"Hello, Carla, I'm Dr. Eugene Brooks. How are you feeling?"

"I'm feeling better."

"Has the nurse been in to check your head?"

"She was in here a couple of hours ago, but I don't recall her checking my head. All she did was write down my vitals and check the machines."

"I'll take a look while I'm here."

"Sure," I replied.

Dr. Eugene Brooks stood beside me and removed the bandage. "Are you having any dizzy spells?"

"No."

"You're not feeling faint or having trouble breathing?"

"No."

"That's good. I would like to send you for another CT scan, just to make sure there isn't any swelling in the cranium. Are you having any abdominal pain?"

"It's a little sore, but nothing I can't handle."

"That's good. Sometimes when you have a baby like this, it can be somewhat uncomfortable, but to reassure you, it will go away in time. Just try to stay rested and off your feet for the next six weeks," Dr. Brooks noted.

"Well, okay, I'll do my best." I saw Tim look at the floor and then back at me, the muscle in his neck twitching, which is only something he does when he's nervous or upset.

"Well, if there's nothing else, I'll send the nurse in to take you for your CT scan."

"Actually," I blurted out, "my husband was just about to tell me something you told him when he came to the hospital yesterday."

"Oh, what was that?"

"I don't know, you came into the room just now and he didn't get to finish telling me."

Before the doctor could respond, his name came over the intercom. "Dr. Brooks, *code blue* in N108. *Code blue* in room N108," a woman ordered over the intercom.

"Sorry, I must go." The doctor quickly ran out the door before he could say anything more.

I looked at my husband, his eyes wide. "What is it?" I asked.

"I'll be right back," he replied and quickly bolted out of the room.

I stared at the doorway confused by Tim and the doctor's quick departure.

Minutes had passed and still no Tim. Just the sounds of people rushing down the hall outside my door.

Thirty minutes later, a nurse with dark hair appeared inside the doorway with a wheelchair. "Dr. Brooks wants me to take you for some tests," the nurse stated.

"Oh, okay," I mumbled, feeling disappointed that Tim hadn't come back after rushing out of the room.

Chapter 4

When I returned an hour later, Tim still wasn't in the room. I couldn't believe that he was avoiding the conversation which he started. I tried hard to think what it could be about, but nothing came to mind. I'd just have to wait until he came back to ask him. I lowered the bed and closed my eyes.

I wasn't sure how long I was asleep when my friend Veronica came into the room, carrying a bouquet of pink roses, my favorite.

"Hey, you. How are you feeling?" Not waiting for a response, she walked to the window and set the vase on the ledge.

"That must be the most popular question in this hospital!" I snapped. I wasn't sure why I was in a sour mood; wait, yes I did know why—Tim.

"Yeah, sorry. You must get asked that often?"

"Too much in fact. How does one usually feel when they're in a hospital?" I barked again.

"I guess you're right, duh. No one would be here if they felt good."

"Sorry, I don't mean to sound snippy," I replied, hitting the button on the bed to sit up.

"No, that's fine," Veronica waved her hand in the air. "After what you went through yesterday, no one would expect you to be chipper."

I smiled, "It's good to have you here."

Veronica walked back to the bed, giving me a long hug, "I talked to Tim earlier and he said you were getting some tests done so I thought I'd wait and come later."

"When did you talk to him?"

"Oh, around ten-thirty this morning."

That had to be right after he ran out of the room, which told me he was still here when I went for my CT scan. "What time is it now?" I asked.

"Going on one. I decided to call the school and take a personal day. I couldn't bring myself to go into work. Besides, I'd rather be here visiting with you. Oh, before I forget, I brought your purse from the classroom."

"Thanks, you can just set it in the drawer for now. I'm glad you came in to see me," I said; yet, I was still disappointed that Tim hadn't returned.

"Like anything would keep me from seeing you." She opened the drawer next to the bed and stuffed my purse inside. "So, were you able to see the baby?" she asked.

"Yes, I did. She's so beautiful. I can't believe it finally happened. I'm finally a *Mom*." Just saying those three letters, again, made me feel all warm inside.

"I know. I was so worried about you. I won't lie to you, but seeing you lying on the floor yesterday, like I did, scared me. I didn't know what to do for you. I couldn't help you, and it frightened me. I was just thankful the paramedics arrived within minutes after I called," Veronica said, wiping a tear from her cheek.

"Me too. Thank you for getting help so quickly. I don't know what I would have done if you hadn't pick up the phone. If you weren't in the office." I reached out and squeezed my friend's hand. "Have you seen my baby?"

"I stopped by and saw her through the glass. You're right, she's beautiful," Veronica replied.

My friend then asked about the tubes and wires, and I filled her in as best as I could with what the nurse had told me. We chatted until the same dark-haired nurse came in, telling Veronica visiting hours were over ten minutes ago. That she could come back later this evening between six and eight. Veronica nodded and waited for the nurse to leave the room.

"Well, I guess I need to leave you now. I'll stop back in later or tomorrow. Do you know when you'll be released?"

"No, not yet. I'll have to talk to the doctor when I see him again."

Veronica leaned over and hugged me one last time.

"Hey before you leave, do you know where Tim went?" I asked.

"No, I haven't seen him. Maybe he had to take care of something and will be back when he's done."

"Yeah, maybe you're right. He may have had some work to finish up."

"I'll stop in later unless you hear anything different from the doctor, like he wants you to rest more or something."

I waved goodbye to my friend and reached for the phone next to the bed. I needed to call Tim and see where he was. I wished he was here with me. I didn't care what the doctor had told him; I just wanted him close to me.

The call went straight to voicemail.

~ ~ ~ ~ ~

Later that night, I woke when Tim slowly opened the door to my room and tiptoed in. Although he was trying to be quiet, trying hard not to wake me, he failed. Not that I was in a deep sleep or anything.

I switched on the light beside the bed. "Where have you been?" I demanded in a whisper.

He turned towards me, "I had some things to take care of at the office; besides they had taken you for tests, and I thought it was a good time to slip away."

"But you've been gone all day. Oh, well. I'm glad you're back now," I reconciled.

"Of course, why wouldn't I come back?"

"I don't know, just seems like you have something on your mind and have been trying to avoid telling me."

"I wasn't trying to avoid you, just needed time to clear my head, that's all." He sat down next to me.

"Well, do you want to talk about what we didn't finish earlier?"

"I guess we need to talk about this sooner or later."

I positioned myself up and studied his face. "So, what did you need to tell me?"

"When I came to the hospital after I got the call about you, Dr. Brooks had told me he had to..." he paused, swallowed.

"He had to what? What happened?" I questioned, my heart pounding in my chest.

He sighed and wiped the sweat from his hands onto his khakis, "I guess there was severe internal bleeding when you went into surgery; they had to do a cesarean to save the baby," Tim swallowed again, staring at my face.

"So this was why you've been so quiet and distant?" I couldn't shake the feeling that he was lying to me, that there was more to the story than he was telling me. Was he afraid I'd do something unthinkable? Although I'd gotten professional help, I knew it still crossed his mind, what I did last year.

Chapter 5

The following morning, Tim left and said he'd be back in a few hours. The conversation we had late last night saddened me, but I didn't want to worry about what I couldn't change. I knew the doctor had to perform some kind of surgery to get my baby safely out of me. So, why would this bother Tim so much? Did he honestly still worry about what I might do to myself? I pushed the thought to the back of my mind.

I grabbed the remote off the nightstand and turned on the TV. I flipped through the channels until I came to a news station. The reporter was talking about gas prices rising, and some of the Chicago schools being shut down. I was relieved when I found out my job wouldn't be affected.

We lived in the south suburbs, away from downtown Chicago. Although, I did feel remorse for the teachers who wouldn't have a job once school started again in the fall.

A young nurse I hadn't seen before came into the room. She didn't look much taller than me, maybe five-four or five-five at the most. She had bright red hair that was cut short into a bob. "So, how are you feeling this morning?" the nurse sang.

"Better," I half shrugged, noticing the name on her ID and how it didn't really fit her appearance.

"Has Dr. Brooks or Dr. Shaffer been in to see you this morning?" Angie asked.

"No, not yet."

"I'll give them both a call to go over your test results and see when you'll be released," Angie concluded.

"Released?" I questioned.

"Yes, the insurance company doesn't allow patients to stay more than a couple of days, unless of course there are problems. It will all depend on the CT scan they took of your head yesterday."

"Oh, I see. And my baby?"

"Your baby will have to stay for quite a while longer. Babies need to weigh as close to five pounds as possible and continue to put on weight before they can be released. She'll also have to breathe on her own; her heart rate will have to stay normal; and she'll also have to eat without the feeding tube."

"Can't I stay here, is what I meant?"

"No, I'm afraid not. They only allow parents that live two to three hours away from the hospital to stay here until the baby is released. I'm sorry. The hospital also requires you and your husband to watch some videos that go over what to expect when you can take your baby home. There are pamphlets about classes you'll need to attend as well to help you both know how to take care of your preemie."

"Of course, I understand. I should know that, right?" I frowned.

"Well, not always, unless you're a nurse or know someone who's in the medical field. Some new mothers find things out as they go along. I have two children and wished they had come with a manual. Both of my children are very different from one another. My first child had colic and wouldn't sleep unless you were holding her for the first six months, but my second baby was as calm as could be. He'd sleep anywhere and never fussed."

"How old are your children?"

"Mary Anne is seven and Nicholas is five."

"Those are wonderful ages. I teach second graders."

"You do? Where?"

"At Haven Elementary, in Homer Glen," I added with a smile. Even though I was glad to have Mya, I missed my students. I missed teaching them.

"That's where my kids go. In fact my daughter came home last night and told me about her friend, Samantha."

"Samantha Berkley?" I questioned, taking a guess, as it was the only Samantha I knew.

"Yes, I do believe that's her last name. Mary Anne goes on and on about her. They play together at recess every day. *But,* the thing that was different this time, was she told me about the bruises up and down Samantha's arm. When I asked her from what, she just repeated to me what Samantha had said."

"What was that?"

"Samantha said she'd fallen off her bike. I didn't think anything of it until my friend Carol who lives next door to them, called and asked if I had heard about the Berkley's abusing their daughter and that they were arrested. When I said I hadn't, she filled me in on what had happened."

So, I was right. Samantha is being abused, or was. "So, she's all right now? She's been taken out of that house?"

"As far as I know, yes. Thank goodness too. Some people out there just don't deserve to have children, ya' know?"

"Yes, I do and I agree," I replied, nodding.

I, for the first time since my baby had been born, felt relieved. Samantha was a bright student and worked hard. I remember a few times whispering in Samantha's ear not to try so hard to please me. I told her that she was very smart, and she was doing great with the projects I was giving her. My heart warmed every time I saw a smile come across Samantha's face.

Another thought came to me that I'd forgotten. A while back, I had reached out my hand and touched Samantha's shoulder giving it a gentle squeeze. The look on her face as she winced and pulled away from my loving touch made me question her story. At the time, I hadn't thought much about it, but now I knew the truth.

"Well, everything looks good. I'll give the doctor a call to come and check on you," the nurse noted.

"Okay, thanks. It was nice talking to you."

"You too, Carla. Take care." Angie padded out the door and down the hall.

A couple of hours later, Dr. Brooks came in to see me and told me that the results looked good, but thought I should stay another day or two, depending on how I felt.

Although it had occurred to me that Dr. Shaffer, my OB/GYN doctor, hadn't come to see me since my arrival, I neglected nor did I question why he hadn't. I suppose deep down, I trusted Dr. Brooks more with Mya and myself than I did with Dr. Shaffer because he had saved both our lives.

After he left the room, I called the nurse in and asked if I could visit with my daughter. The nurse replied that she'd have to ask the doctor first and would let me know. Several minutes later, she returned, helping me into a wheelchair.

Outside Mya's room, the nurse draped a gown over the front of me and wheeled me inside the room. I washed my hands in the sink as instructed by the nurse and then she moved me beside the radiant warmer also known as a neonatal incubator.

"I can't let you hold her, but you can sit next to her. I'll stay right here with you, in case something should go wrong," the nurse said.

I took my eyes off Mya and looked at the nurse with a confused look on my face, but instead of asking, I nodded and turned back towards my daughter.

A world of emotions flowed through my body. I had dreamed of the day I would have a baby, and now as I sat here and looked at her, I prayed that she would survive. That she would get to come home with me.

My daughter was tiny and was as long as my forearm. I wished I could touch her—hold my beautiful girl.

"Don't give up, Mya Ann. Please fight for Mommy," I whispered. Tears rolled down my cheeks as I watched my daughter fighting for her life.

On the way back to the room, I noticed the small-engraved plaque beside Mya's door that read N108. My mind flashed back to yesterday when the doctor and Tim had bolted out of the room. The two words being broadcasted over the intercom made me gasp.

Code Blue.

Chapter
6

I had to quiet my mind as it raced with the information I'd just found out. Mya had stopped breathing. She'd almost died! Yet, Tim never said a word to me. He just ran out of the room behind the doctor and neglected to tell me what was going on. I had no clue until I saw her room number. I knew he was protecting me; he had good reasons to do so. Especially, after what I put him through last year.

$$\sim \sim \sim \sim \sim$$

It wasn't until the following morning when I woke with him in the chair next to me that I decided to set my findings aside for now. I could tell by the look of him that he was suffering inside with what had happened. There was no need to bring it up, not right now.

After eating the bland hospital food they gave me for breakfast, Tim wheeled me into the elevator and pushed the button for the fifth floor. He said he wanted to take me to meet someone. When the elevator doors opened, he led me down the hall and into the children's ward.

"Mrs. Michaels!" Samantha cried out as we entered the room.

I smiled when I heard Samantha's voice and glanced up at Tim. Without thinking of the pain I'd been having, I quickly stood and walked to the side of her bed. I couldn't help but wonder how Tim knew that Samantha was one of my students.

She scooted to the edge of the bed and wrapped her arms around my waist. The embrace startled me at first, and then I softened. It wasn't until I pulled away that I got a good look at Samantha. I gasped as I saw the bruises covering her face and the cast on her arm.

Oh, dear God, I thought, knowing better than to speak the words aloud. Even though I was told Samantha was being abused, seeing her like this sickened me. All this time I'd had reason to believe Samantha was being abused. I, of course, didn't want to believe her own parents could do that to her. I saw for the first time as I stood there, poor beautiful Samantha, bruised and abused.

"Hello, Samantha, how are you doing?" I asked, and then felt stupid for asking. *Look at her, how in the hell do you think she's doing?* I scolded myself.

"I'm good now that you're here. I missed you, Mrs. Michaels. When are you coming back to school?" she questioned.

I sat in the chair next to the bed, "Not for a while, sweetie. I have some mending to do," I replied, patting my stomach where the baby once was.

"What does *mending* mean?"

"It means, I need to heal and feel better before I can go back to school."

"Oh, like me," Samantha replied, holding up her cast.

"Yes, I guess you can put it that way," I half smiled, and then nodded in agreement.

"Where is your baby? Mr. Michaels told me you had a girl. What did you name her?"

I glanced up at Tim with a confused look on my face. *When had he met Samantha? When had he talked to her?* I realized I didn't know my husband as well as I thought I did. Although it did dawn on me that he had to have known she was here, why else would he have brought me to see her?

"Pat Atkins and I had to come here and ask her some questions yesterday. She asked if you were my wife because our last names are the same. She also asked where you went, so I told her about the baby."

"Oh, she's your case now?" I asked.

Tim nodded.

I started to ask another question, but decided to wait until later. I didn't want to ask them in front of Samantha.

"Well, to answer your question, my baby, Mya Ann, is sleeping. She isn't well enough to visit yet," I frowned and looked down at my lap.

"Don't be sad, Mrs. Michaels. Does she have a cold or something? I've had colds before, but they don't stay for very long. I'm sure hers will go away, just like mine did. You just have to give her some soup and let her sleep," Samantha said, knowingly.

A smile appeared on my face as I looked back up at Samantha. *The questions and answers kids came up with,* I thought and started to laugh. "I guess you can say that." Knowing I couldn't and wouldn't explain the truth to her.

"So, what is it you're coloring?" I pointed towards the table.

"A dog," she replied. "The nice nurse gave me a coloring book and some crayons."

"Did she now? Well, she must know how much you like to color."

Samantha shrugged her shoulders and sat back against the pillow, letting out a sigh.

Silence filled the air, which made me uncomfortable. I didn't know what to say to this child I'd only known for seven months. In class, it was different, but outside of school, I just felt…unsure. I didn't want to overstep my boundaries as a teacher, but here, now, looking at my student, I wanted to reach out and take her pain away, to protect her from anyone else hurting her, again. Was I right to feel this way about a child that wasn't mine?

I reached out, grasped Samantha's hand in mine and squeezed gently, then looked at her face. Tears slid down Samantha's bruised cheek and splattered on the white sheet, leaving a wet circle.

With my free hand, I wiped the wetness away with my thumb. "It'll be all right, Samantha. Mr. Michaels will make sure nothing like this ever happens to you again, I promise."

Samantha batted her eyes at me, trying to stop the tears from escaping. "I just don't want my mommy and daddy to be mad at me. It was my fault for breaking the vase. I shouldn't *have runned* into the house. They tell me never to run in the house, or I will be punished. I was just so excited about the picture I made in school, and you said you wanted to hang it up because it was so beautiful," Samantha explained, sniffling.

"Oh, sweetie. It's not your fault. Don't ever blame yourself for what they did to you. You don't deserve to be hit, no one does."

"But if I hadn't *runned* into the house and knocked over the vase, then I wouldn't *had* made my mommy and daddy so mad at me."

"Samantha, you couldn't have known what your parents would do to you."

"But I always seem to make them mad at me. I try to be a good girl and do what they say, but sometimes I guess…I guess I forget things," she said as she started to cry.

"You are a good girl. Don't you ever think differently. I'd never get mad at you. You're a great student, and so kind and smart too."

Samantha's face glistened from the words I spoke. "Would you like to color a picture with me?" Samantha asked, using the back of her hand to wipe more of the wetness away.

"Yes, I'd like that very much," I replied with a smile.

I couldn't understand how Samantha just told me what her mommy and daddy did to her, and then as if nothing had been said, asked me to color with her. I knew from teaching that children could be remarkably resilient.

I grabbed the arm of the chair, pulled myself up onto the bed, and sat beside Samantha. I pulled the table close to us and started coloring on the opposite page.

Almost an hour had passed when Samantha laid her head back and closed her eyes. She told me she was feeling sleepy.

Once outside the room, Tim knelt down to face me, but I didn't feel like talking. I wrapped my arms around my husband. I didn't want to let go; but more than anything, I didn't want anything bad to happen to Samantha.

Tim kissed the top of my head, stood, and stepped back behind the wheelchair, making our way into the elevator. I was feeling tired and asked to be taken back to my room so I could sleep.

The rest of the afternoon and evening, I had made several trips to NICU to see Mya and then laid in my bed, thinking about Samantha. I was relieved, yet scared of what she still had to go through, but hoped Tim would make everything better and keep her safe.

Chapter 7

The following morning, Tim took me to see Samantha. When we returned to the third floor, my friend Ashley Teodora was sitting in the hall outside my room. My eyes immediately fell on Ashley's blonde hair that had once cascaded down her back; it was now cut short and sat just above the shoulders.

"Ashley, what are you doing here? I thought you were coming this weekend. And what'd you do to your hair?" I asked, sounding shocked and excited all at the same time.

"Hey, girlfriend," Ashley replied as she stood. "Every couple of years I get my hair cut and donate it to children with cancer. And besides, I wanted to surprise you and come see the new arrival." Ashley said as she bent down to give me a hug.

"I'm so glad you came. Tim just took me to see one of my students who's in the hospital." I didn't want to go into detail with what had happened to Samantha, unless of course, Ashley asked, but she didn't.

"The nurse is in the room with your daughter so I thought I'd wait out here for you to return," she noted.

"Ashley, I thought you'd be here later today," Tim stated.

"Yeah, well I decided to get a head start this morning and arrived here sooner than I thought I would. I stopped at the house first. When I saw all the accumulated newspapers in the driveway, I figured no one had been home in a while. Your neighbor Deanna saw me and said no one had been at the house in days, but wasn't sure what had happened," Ashley said. "Then I remembered, you were probably still in the hospital so I had called and they said that you were still here."

I looked up at Tim with a baffled look. "You didn't tell me she was coming early."

"That's why it's called a surprise, besides I think you could use the company while Mya's in the hospital," Tim added.

I nodded, feeling too tired to get into a conversation about him knowing Ashley was coming to see me.

"Do either of you want to head to the cafeteria for something to eat?" Tim asked.

"That sounds great, I'm actually starving again," Ashley replied. "I had a long drive and didn't sleep so well last night."

"How about you, hon? Are you feeling up to eating?" Tim asked.

"Yeah, I guess I could go with the two of you since Mya is sleeping. Can we see her before we head to my room on the way back?"

"Of course we can," Tim assured me.

I pretty much kept my thoughts to myself as the three of us made our way to the cafeteria. Not only was I thinking of Mya, but Samantha wasn't far from my thoughts. I'd never understood what it was that Tim did in his job. I knew what some attorneys did, but never really asked my husband what it was like being a Child Advocate and working with children services. We talked about work from time to time, but I hadn't asked him what it was like to be around children that are or were being abused. I wondered how he handled it emotionally. He seemed good at keeping his feelings to himself.

In all the years as a teacher, Samantha was the first child I'd ever felt close to like this. I cared for all my students, but there was something about Samantha I couldn't define. Maybe it was because she was easy to please and made my job as a teacher more fulfilling.

My body shook from images of Samantha with her bruises and cast on her thin arm. *How could anyone do that to their own child?* I thought. I couldn't imagine ever hitting my child just because they made me mad. I'd ask Tim later what Samantha's options were and who'd take care of her now.

Part of me felt bad for never asking Tim about his day-to-day job. Did that make me a bad wife? Should I have asked those kinds of questions? But then, if I heard him talk about all those abused children, how would that affect me now? Would I be a different person than who I was today? I wasn't sure. I said a silent prayer inside my head, praying that Samantha would stay safe.

~ ~ ~ ~ ~

Back in the room, Ashley filled me in on her five year-old daughter Lily Rose and talked about other things that were filling up her time.

"Well, I'm glad you're here. It's nice to see you again. Where's Lily?" Tim asked.

Ashley and I both gave Tim a look of confusion. "Weren't you listening?" Ashley laughed. "My mom said she'd keep her while I was away visiting. She didn't think it'd be a good idea to bring her along. You know with the new baby and all."

Tim nodded.

We all turned when the door to the room opened and Dr. Brooks came walking in.

"Well, how is my patient feeling this afternoon?"

"I'm doing fine," I replied.

"That's great to hear." He flipped through my chart then added, "All your scans look good, no swelling or damage around the brain. I want to do a quick check-over and then if everything looks great, I don't see any reason for you to continue your stay in the hospital."

"Oh, okay," I pouted, feeling disappointed that I had to leave my daughter here while I went home.

"You don't seem excited to leave?" Dr. Brooks questioned.

"Well, it's just that…" I paused, noticing that all eyes were on me. "It's just that Mya is here and… and I don't know why I can't stay," I said, sounding like I was on the verge of crying.

"I see, well, I do apologize for any inconvenience. You can come visit your baby anytime you want. Although, I do suggest you have someone drive you to and from the hospital. It may be several weeks before you can drive yourself."

I nodded at the doctor, and then Tim spoke, "When will she be released?"

"Actually, right now," Dr. Brooks announced, after he replaced the bandage on my forehead.

Before Tim could respond, Ashley jumped in. "I'll take her home, Tim, if you have things to do."

"Thanks, that would be great. I actually have this new case I'm working on and have to meet with a colleague in an hour to go over everything."

"Well, then it's settled. I'll take Carla home, you go and finish what you need to do," Ashley insisted.

I scowled at Tim, giving him a slow disapproving headshake.

"Do you need or want a prescription for any pain you may be having? I can give you a script for Percocet or something with codeine?" Dr. Brooks asked.

"No, I can't have codeine. I'm allergic to it," I informed him.

Dr. Brooks thumbed through the chart in his hand, "Oh, yes, I see that here. I'll give you a script for Percocet, which doesn't have codeine." The doctor pulled a prescription pad from his white coat pocket and scribbled on it, then handed it to Tim. "Do you have any other questions before you're discharged?" Dr. Brooks asked, looking from me to Tim.

"No," Tim and I both replied at the same time, making Ashley snicker.

"All right then," Dr. Eugene Brooks smiled, "I'll let the nurse know you're ready to go and make sure she gives you the information you need about NICU and taking care of your baby before you leave."

I nodded.

"Do you need me to do anything before I go?" Tim asked.

"No, I'm fine. Besides, I have Ashley here to help me if I need something."

"Okay, then I'll see you when I get home tonight. I'll stop at the pharmacy and pick-up your prescription," he said, holding up the piece of paper the doctor had just given him. He knelt down, kissed me, said goodbye to Ashley, and left the room.

Ten minutes after Tim left, a nurse entered the room. "So I hear you're going home?"

Ashley sat back and listened to the conversation between the nurse and me.

"Yeah," I frowned.

"I know you're not too thrilled about leaving, but just keep in mind that Mya will be in good hands."

"I know you told me that before. It's just... just that I wish she could come with me and not have to stay here."

"In time she will. She just has to get stronger."

I agreed and looked at Ashley.

The nurse then handed me a form. "I need you to sign this for your release."

I grabbed the paper and pen, signed my name and handed it back. The nurse gave me a couple more papers to read over and keep. "This form is to let you know what to expect with the C-section you had. It states what you should and shouldn't do. Get plenty of rest and take care of yourself."

"You had a C-section?"

"That's what I've been told, yes."

Ashley looked at the nurse, "I'll make sure she doesn't over do it." The nurse then handed me a bag and told me what was in it.

"There's a hotline you can call if you have any questions about your preemie and what to expect when your baby does come home. Please take the time to watch the video and read the pamphlets I have given you. They really will help."

"I will," I said.

"Good. Once you're finished getting dressed, I can take you to spend some time with Mya before you leave."

"Okay, thank you."

The nurse turned and walked out the door, closing it behind her.

"Where are your clothes so I can help you get dressed?"

"I think they're in the cabinet over there." Ashley turned her head in the direction I was pointing and stood. She walked over and opened the door to the bureau; there was nothing in there. "There are no clothes," she said.

"I guess they must have thrown them out when I was taken into surgery."

"Why would they do that?"

"Most likely because there was blood on them."

"What? You never told me that."

"Well, it's not something I wanted to tell you over the phone, Ash."

My friend sat down next to the bed. "I'm here now if you want to talk to me," Ashley said.

"I was at school, my class had just ended, and I started having some sharp pain," I continued with the story as she sat wide-eyed, and listening to every word.

"Oh, my God, I am so sorry, Carla. I can't imagine what you were going through. And I take it the bandage is from where you hit your head?"

"Yes. It happened so fast, the next thing I remember was waking up here and Tim sitting beside me. He was the one that told me about the C-section they had to do."

"Why didn't the doctor tell you?"

"I don't know, maybe Tim told him not to."

"I guess I can understand his reasons. I mean you both have been trying for years to have a baby and then something like this happens and now…" Ashley stopped in mid-sentence. "Let me run to your house and get you some clothes."

"You don't have to do that; I'll just wear this gown home."

"At least let me go down to the gift shop and see if they have any sweat pants or something you can wear."

"Fine, I know better than to argue with you," I laughed.

Ashley left the room and returned fifteen minutes later. She had bought a pair of jogging pants and a T-shirt from the gift shop. She helped me get dressed. She found a wheelchair in the hall, helped me into it, and then we headed to NICU.

Ashley stood behind me as we both stared through the window. An alarm sounded and three other nurses along with Dr. Brooks came running down the hall and into Mya's room. Ashley pulled me away from the window and took me down the hall where I couldn't see what was happening.

"What are you doing?" I hissed.

"Carla, I'm sorry, but you don't need to be watching what they are doing in there."

"But I need to see her." I grabbed the armrest to push myself up.

"Carla, please sit down before you hurt yourself!"

Ashley stood in front of me, keeping me from getting out of the chair. "Don't tell me what I should do! She needs me. My baby girl needs her mother!" I snapped at her.

She knelt down in front of me and whispered, "They are working on her. I'm sure as soon as they're done the doctor will come and talk to you." Her eyes searched my face that I knew had been beautiful and serene one minute, then beat red with anger the next, but my friend wasn't going to let me move from that spot and head into the room.

"Please stay seated, Carla. I'm asking you nicely," Ashley demanded through gritted teeth.

Tears cascaded down my face as I sat back into the wheelchair, putting my face in my hands. In what felt like hours, but was only twenty minutes or so, the doctor came out of the room and saw me sitting off to the side.

Our eyes connected and I could tell by the look on his face that the news wasn't good. His Adams apple stuck out of his neck as he swallowed hard and then walked over to where we were.

"Come with me," Dr. Brooks said. Ashley turned the wheelchair around and followed him down the hall. He stopped and opened a door to the left and motioned us to go inside. He shut the door and walked passed us to a chair behind a desk and sat. He folded his hands on top of the desk while keeping his eyes on me. My friend grabbed my hand and squeezed.

Chapter 8

The doctor moved his eyes from me to Ashley. "There's no easy way to say this. Your baby has severe respiratory distress syndrome. Long-term complications may develop because of too much oxygen and high pressures delivered to the lungs; there will be periods when the brain or other organs do not receive enough oxygen. I'm sorry but there's nothing much we can do for her, but to wait."

"How long?" I asked without blinking.

"Twenty-four to forty-eight hours and that would be pushing it. Mrs. Michaels, I do suggest you call your husband and spend some time with your baby. She may not make it through the night."

Ashley gasped from the doctor's words and then put her arm around me. Over all the years we'd been friends, it didn't take a genius to know when to comfort your friend. I needed someone to hold onto, and my friend was here for me. To cry for the loss of my baby, knowing deep down in my heart, Tim should be the one here with me, holding me, but he wasn't…

Even after what the doctor had said, I was sent home. With the chances of infection, neither Tim nor I were allowed in to see Mya. I could watch from the glass window as nurses and doctors were the only ones allowed in the room.

~ ~ ~ ~ ~

Ashley and I went to the hospital early the next morning and then came back home. We both figured we'd eat something and then head back to see Mya who was still staying strong, even after what the doctor had told us.

I was leaning against the counter looking out the window in the kitchen when Ashley came down from upstairs.

"Hey, Carla, is everything all right?"

I turned around slowly and looked at Ashley. "I'm good. Just thinking about Mya and wishing things were different."

"I know you do, but she will get stronger and healthier and be home before you know it." Ashley glided over to where I stood and stretched out her arms. I didn't hesitate for a second and went in for a hug. I wept as my best friend held me in her arms. When I pulled back, my face was red and puffy. Ashley released her hands, grabbed the box of Kleenex from the counter, and held it out for me.

"Would you like me to make us something to eat?" Ashley asked.

"I'm not that hungry."

"I know you're not, but you do have to keep up your strength for your baby. You don't need to end up back in the hospital," Ashley protested.

I shrugged my shoulders.

"Let me make us some soup."

"Okay," I replied.

Ashley made her way to the pantry and searched through the cans on the shelf. She came back with a large can of Campbell's chicken and rice and a bag of crackers.

After serving the soup, we both sat at the kitchen table. I took a couple of bites and then set my spoon back in the bowl.

"Can I talk to you about something?" Ashley asked.

"Of course, you can always talk to me."

"I know, but with everything going on, I don't want to burden you with my problems."

My head sprung up and my eyes narrowed on Ashley's face. "What is it?"

Taking in a deep breath, she swallowed then spoke. "Rob and I have just hit a hard spot in our relationship, that's all. I guess I'm not sure if I want to marry Rob. It doesn't seem to be working out."

"Tell me what happened?"

"I guess I'm just wondering if marriage is for everyone. I'm sorry; it's nothing that I can't work out. Besides, I'm here for you, not for me."

"Really, Ash? I thought we knew each other better than that. We've always talked and shared our problems and worries," I noted.

She shrugged her shoulders, "It's really nothing. I'm sorry for saying anything at all, really. Just forget I ever said anything."

I wasn't sure where to go with this so I directed my question elsewhere to find out what was bothering my best friend, hoping she would tell me more. "Does your mom know you both are having problems?" I asked.

"Nope, I couldn't bring myself to tell her. I just wanted to get away, and since I was coming out here, I thought why not come early? I was going to bring Lily with me, but my mom said it would be best to have her stay with her, you know because of you having the baby and all. So, I went home and packed a bag and left. I plan on telling her, after Rob and I talk."

"Yeah, that's probably a good idea." Although I had no clue what their problems were.

"So, do you have any advice to give your best friend?"

Again, after not getting her to talk to me, I had to just tell her what I always believed in. "I don't know about advice, but I believe things happen for a reason. Just think about if you were married, would this problem be an issue?"

"I guess you're right, that's a very good point. I just wonder if I'll ever find my Mr. Right."

"Sure you will. He's out there somewhere. You just have to be in the right place at the right time."

"Easy for you to say. You already have a great guy."

I bowed my head. "Yeah, I don't know what I'd do without him. Normally, I'm good at reading his face, but lately, I don't know, it's been somewhat hard. I have no idea what he's thinking. I know he has a new case he's been working on, and with that and Mya. I guess I could see how he could be distracted."

"What case could be more important than Mya?"

"There's a young girl—she's a student of mine and for a while now I've had my suspicions she was being abused by someone, possibly one of her parents or both. Anyway, the day before you showed up, Tim took me to see her. I didn't even know she was in the hospital. She had bruises all over and a cast on her arm. After we visited, I asked Tim about what happened. He said he couldn't tell me a whole lot, but what he did say was that both of her parents had been abusing her. I'm just glad she's out of that house and somewhere where she won't be harmed anymore."

"Oh, that's so sad, Carla. Well, I'm glad to hear she's safe now. Hopefully that will be over soon and you both can focus on Mya."

"I didn't know Tim had these kinds of cases. I never asked him about his work. I'm just sad that it's one of my students. I don't know how parents can do that to their child and think that it's okay," I said.

"I feel the same way," Ashley replied as she glanced around the table. She pointed towards the newspaper sitting beside me. "Can I see that paper for a minute?"

I slid the newspaper over to her. She scanned over the front-page article. There was a photo of a motel and she read the caption. "Holy Hell!" Ashley blurted out.

"What is it?"

"This motel here." She laid the paper down and pointed to the picture."

"Yeah, what about it?"

"I stopped there to spend the night on my way here. It looks just as creepy in the photo as it did in-person."

"What's it say about the motel?"

"Well, it says here that a young woman came running out into traffic on Interstate 80/90, acting all hysterical. A man driving a red BMW swerved, just missing her and pulled off the highway. The woman told the—name not mentioned—man that her husband had been murdered. He called 911 from his cell.

When the local police arrived, she explained that she heard a noise outside the bathroom window and after noticing her husband was gone, she followed the sound and saw the owner of the motel digging a hole behind the room where they had been sleeping, and her husband was lying on the ground. She said that she'd freaked out and just started running, praying that the lady wasn't coming after her.

When the police went back to the motel, an older woman answered the door looking as if she had been just woken up. While one of the officers was questioning the owner, another was scoping out the property and found over ten crosses staked in the ground. An hour later, a team of forensics were digging up the graves and found more than twenty male corpses—possibly within the past five to ten years—including the woman's husband who was just buried. The lady that owned the motel was arrested for multiple counts of manslaughter."

"Oh, shit," I replied.

Ashley looked up at me as if she'd never heard me swear before.

"What are you smirking about?"

"You just said, *shit*. I've never heard you say anything bad like that before."

"Oh, well sometimes it comes out. You're right I don't normally say it, but it kind of fit the moment."

"The moment," Ashley laughed, which made me laugh. "It's so good to hear you laughing again," Ashley said.

"Yeah, it feels good too."

"I guess it's a good thing that I'm female, otherwise I wouldn't be here right now. It seems this woman who owns the motel didn't like men at all."

"I have to say you're right, Ashley."

"Not to change the subject, but I've been wanting to talk to you about what happened last year. You know when you went in for help."

My eyes went from Ashley to my hands in my lap. "What do you want to know?"

"I worry about you, and I know that sometimes life can be rough and dish out some harsh lessons. But when you were in that place, what exactly were you feeling?"

My voice was low, but Ashley could still make out the words I was saying. "To put it in a short story, I wanted to end my life."

Ashley took in a sharp breath; she had never expected me, her best friend, to say and feel that way. "Why, sweetie? What was so bad that you didn't want to live?"

I looked at Ashley and studied her face before continuing. "You have to promise not to tell Tim."

"Okay, I promise." She squeezed my hand.

"First I want you to know that I love him. I really do, but sometimes it isn't enough."

"I'm not sure I follow."

"This man, he does everything for me and whatever I want he will find a way to make it happen. But after the last four miscarriages, I didn't think he could ever give me what I really wanted."

"A baby?"

"Yes. Don't get me wrong, I do love him and he does make me happy, but if Mya dies there will be nothing he could do to…"

"To what?"

"To make me want to live."

"Carla, you don't mean that? There's more to life than having a baby. Besides you can always adopt."

"It's not the same."

"I'm sorry if I sound cold, but Carla, you have an amazing man and I can tell that he would give his life for you. Do you honestly think that ending your life will fix everything?" Her voice grew louder. "Do you have any clue what that would do to him or me for that matter? We love you and want you to be happy, but that's something you will have to find inside of yourself. No one can make you happy or give you happiness." Ashley looked furious.

I sat there saying nothing, just looking down at my hands as if I was being scolded like a child.

"I'm sorry, Carla. I didn't mean for all that to come out. Maybe I was being a little harsh on you. Say something, please."

Silence sat between us as if neither of us had anything to say. We'd known each other our whole lives. We went to elementary, middle school, and high school together and hung out every weekend. We knew each other better than we knew ourselves, but this was something my friend Ashley never knew about me. This was something I had never confided in her. I knew Ashley had never seen this coming. What could I say now that would ease the friction between us? Ashley had already said the words; she couldn't take them back now.

"I knew you wouldn't understand," I replied.

"Help me understand," Ashley whispered.

"You are blessed with Lily, and me, I have nothing."

"What do you mean you have nothing?"

"You think all is well with Tim and me, but you don't know."

"Then why don't you tell me?"

"After I lost the first baby, he was there for me. We comforted each other, but then after the third and fourth loss, he changed. He would stay at work longer, and we stopped having sex like we used to. It was like living with a friend and not a husband. Although, I had also changed, but whenever I wanted to start trying to make another baby, he would give me some kind of excuse why he didn't want to have sex. Tim said it was too early, that we should hold off a while for me to heal. I was so unhappy and didn't know what to do. I felt that ending my life was better than living it. Like I said, I do love him, but sometimes love isn't enough. If Mya dies, I don't know what I will do or how I will go on…" I stopped.

Ashley watched my eyes leave hers and followed them to the doorway of the kitchen, where Tim was standing there listening.

Chapter 9

I wouldn't have said the words that had just came out of my mouth if I'd known Tim had walked through the front door. It wasn't until he stood in the doorway of the kitchen, staring at me with an open mouth that I knew for sure, he'd heard what I said.

I stopped in mid-sentence. A look of horror surfaced on my face. "Tim, when did you get home?" I whispered, my heart pounding beneath my blouse. I never meant for Tim to hear me say those words. I swallowed, waiting for him to say something to me.

"I thought I'd come home for lunch, and see how you were doing."

I said nothing. My eyes fixated on the muscle twitching along his jawline.

Tim asked, "Ashley, can you please leave us alone for a few minutes? I think Carla and I need to talk."

Ashley rose, squeezed my hand, and then padded out of the room and up the stairs. I knew he was waiting to hear the door click shut before approaching me.

He pulled the chair further out from the table and took a seat, "Why haven't you told me about this? Do you hate being with me that much?"

Thoughts of a year ago came flooding back. "Tim…" I paused. "I don't hate you. I have never hated you. I love you, but sometimes I feel lost. Like…like I can't breathe," I whispered.

"My love for you isn't enough? I thought you were fine when you…when you returned home last year. But you weren't, were you?"

"I was, well, at first…then… now… with Mya being as sick as she is. I don't know; it's hard to explain, but this doesn't have to do with not loving you."

"Then we have no other choice but to get you more help," he protested.

"No! I can't leave my Mya!" I snapped, feeling angry all of a sudden.

"*Your* Mya?" His voiced shifted, his forehead creased. "I helped bring her into this world too," he mumbled. "She's as much mine as she is yours," his voice continued to rise. "Besides why are we doing this? Why are we fighting over her when she's the one in the hospital fighting to live?" he slammed his fist on the table, spilling the saltshaker.

Tears cascaded down my face, and then I went into a full-blown bawl. I covered my face with my hands and continued to cry like a child not getting their way.

Tim fell to his knees in front of me, embracing me in his arms, "Oh, Carla. I love you so much. What can I do to show you how much I care for you? To prove that you're my world, and that I can't and don't want to live without you?"

I sobbed in the crevice of his neck. I took a breath every few seconds, making me cough and hiccup at the same time.

He pulled me away and stared at my red tear-streaked face. "Do you want me to take you to the same facility as before?"

"No," I replied, with a sniffle.

"Maybe, it'd be better if we seek some kind of counseling. You know like marriage counseling."

"Maybe," I replied.

"I think it's a start."

"Why do you love me so much?" I questioned.

"I just do. I fell in love with you the moment I saw you in college. I love your smile and the way your eyes shine when you're happy. The way you twist your hair between your fingers when you're nervous and bite your lower lip. I could name a hundred more things about you that I love, but maybe the question is, what made you fall in love with me? Maybe you need to reach inside yourself and find it again? I will do whatever it takes to make our marriage survive, with or without a baby."

I looked into his eyes, "But..."

"But what? What do you want? What are you feeling inside?"

"I don't know why I feel I need to have a baby to fulfill my life with you. Why can't I be okay with the fact I may not be able to have my own child? *If...*"

"Mya is a fighter, she will pull through!"

"And *if* she doesn't?"

"Then we'll go from there. We made it through this before, I know we can make it again."

"This time is different. This time we had a baby, and her name is Mya Ann. Before…there were no names. They didn't get a chance to breathe. To see us as their parent. How is it that you can be so strong and I'm so weak?" I asked.

"I don't know that I am strong, but I have faith that she'll pull through this. And *if* she doesn't, then I believe there is a reason for her not to be here. *But,* we have to stay positive and get you the help you need. I'm not giving up on you or us, for that matter. I know you were in love with me once, and you'll find it again. Please say you'll try?" he pleaded.

"I do love you, Tim, and I'll do whatever needs to be done to get better, I…I promise," I whispered, trying to convince myself that I meant what I said.

"That's all I needed to hear. I love you so much, Carla. Do you feel up to seeing our daughter before I have to go back to work?"

I nodded and wrapped my arms around him. "I'll go let Ashley know and see what she wants to do. I'll need a ride back from the hospital."

Tim stood and stepped back, allowing me to have my space. I left him standing alone in the kitchen with his thoughts.

Chapter 10

I reached out my hand to tap on the door of Ashley's room, but stopped in mid-air. I wasn't sure what my friend would say to me after what had happened downstairs. What would my best friend Ashley think of me, if she knew I thought of death—suicide, sometimes? Would she think less of me, and turn away from me? Or, would she continue to stay by my side and support me through this? I hadn't told anyone about what happened a year ago, until today.

I wasn't sure, but I knew my friend well. If there was anything on Ashley's mind, she'd let you know. Ashley wasn't the kind of person to hold back her thoughts. No! She spoke her mind. You either liked it or you didn't.

I wasn't the speaking-up kind of person. I'd hold my tongue, until I couldn't keep my feelings locked inside anymore, then I'd blow. I went months, sometimes years, holding things inside. I'd eventually let it all out, though; it usually took something tragic before it came spilling out. With everything going on these past few days, I'd let my guard down and released some of what I was feeling inside. I took in a deep breath and tapped on the door.

"Come in," Ashley responded.

I turned the knob and slowly pushed the door open, "Was just wondering if you wanted to come to the hospital with us? Tim has to go back to work in an hour, or maybe you could come by and pick me up when I'm done?"

"Sure, that's no problem. You can call me when you're done and I'll be there."

I nodded and turned to leave.

"Do you want to talk about what happened downstairs?" she asked.

I stopped in my tracks. I'd hoped Ashley wouldn't ask, but now that she had, I knew I wanted to talk. I turned back around, walked to the bed and sat down.

"Tim and I are going to try marriage counseling. He really wants our marriage to work."

"And you don't?"

I thought for a second. *Of course, I wanted our marriage to work, didn't I? I did love Tim. No, I do love him, but? But what? What was I really afraid of? No, I knew I wasn't afraid. I actually didn't know what I wanted, besides a baby of course. That's all I had ever wanted. So, therapy or counseling—whatever people called it—was what we needed to do if we were to make our marriage last.*

"Of course I do," I said, hoping my friend didn't hear the uncertainty in my voice. "I just have some things to sort through and figure out what's important to me."

One time, Tim was all I needed and now…now I guess I wanted more. I'm not sure what has changed, maybe spending the last nine years trying to have a baby. Maybe I let it become my obsession, and I forgot about what it was putting Tim through. I guess, I was only thinking of myself and no one else, I thought.

"That maybe, you were being a little selfish?" Ashley said, to the point.

"Yeah, I guess so. Leave it to you to be honest with me. You never hold back any punches, do you?"

"You know me so well, Carla," Ashley laughed. "I guess..." She paused. "I guess we all have things we need to learn from these days," Ashley replied, looking away.

"You certainly got that right."

"Have you ever given much thought to adopting a child or a baby? I know you said you wanted your own, but there are many children out there that need a home and a family."

"I know, you're right, but my priority is Mya, right now. I'm not going to give up on her!"

"No one said you had to, but you have to stop and look at the big picture, Carla. God has a plan for you, and it may or may not include Mya," Ashley said, touching my hand and holding it firmly, giving me strength. "Trust me when I say this, you have every right to want your own child, but keep in mind that we don't have control over what happens to us. We get what is dished out, but it's our decision and our choice what we do with it. Considering how long I've known you, you're not one to give up. You always find a way to get what you want, and you work hard at it. Just take some time and really think about your life, especially with Tim in mind. He loves you more than you know. Anyone can see that," Ashley smiled. "I envy you, Carla. You have a man who loves you with all his heart and would give you the world. I wish I could find a love like that."

"What about Rob?"

She shrugged," I don't think he's the right guy for me."

"Oh?"

"Ah, it's nothing you need to worry about," she batted her hand in the air. "I'll find love one day. On the other hand, maybe it's just not in my cards. I guess we'll all wait and see what happens down the road."

"And just so you know, I am jealous of what you have."

"Lily?"

"Yes, she's your world, and no man is worth your time if she isn't first on his list."

"You're right," Ashley smiled in agreement.

"Okay, enough of this mushy gushy stuff. I want to go see my baby girl."

"You go, and I'll be waiting for your call. I have some more calls of my own to make so I'll see you later."

"Sounds good to me. How about we go out for dinner tonight since you're leaving on Sunday to go home?" I suggested, mostly because I hadn't felt up to cooking much these days.

"No arguments here," Ashley replied.

"Good." I embraced my friend, and then left the room. I strolled down the stairs and saw Tim waiting by the door.

"Ready to go?" he asked.

"I just need to grab my purse," I replied.

"Make sure you grab a sweater too. It's starting to cool down outside," Tim said.

I nodded and went to retrieve my wool sweater along with my purse.

Once in the car, silence filled the air between us. I stared out the window, watching the houses pass by. My mind was spinning in circles as I thought about everything that had happened moments ago. I wasn't sure what to say to my husband. What could I say after the talk we'd had, and what he'd heard? Besides, Tim getting mad about the way I said Mya was mine; he did seem angry with me. I didn't know if he would be furious with me or continue being the same Tim I've known all these years. It wasn't like we fought all the time. Actually, I couldn't remember us ever really fighting at all. He pretty much gave me whatever I wanted.

For the first time, I'd have to agree with my best friend—I was being selfish. I was putting my needs before Tim's, and he had always done the opposite. Why didn't I realize this before? How did I not see what I was becoming? Right then, I knew I was still in love with him, but I would have to work on showing him that he meant more to me than giving up. I wasn't ready to try to end my life, again. Nor could I even go through with it. I'd need to be strong for Mya; no matter what the outcome was.

Chapter 11

Tim pulled into the parking lot of the hospital and parked the car. I turned towards him and reached my hand out, touching his. "I want us to work," I whispered. My heart was beating fast and hard. I slipped my right hand under my thigh to keep it from shaking.

He smiled, "I do too."

He took his hand from beneath mine and caressed my cheek. I leaned over and kissed him tenderly on the lips.

"I love you, Tim Michaels."

"And I love you, Carla Michaels," he whispered through his lips.

"Please don't leave me," I said. "I'll try to be a better wife and give you what you want and need."

His face softened, as if he were about to cry, but didn't. I kissed him once more and pulled back, his eyes still closed. I touched his cheek with my hand. His eyes slowly opened. I could see the longing in his deep blue eyes, something I hadn't seen in a long time.

"You are a good wife, and you do give me what I want and need," he smiled.

"Shall we go in and see our daughter?" I asked.

He nodded in return.

Outside the car, I tightened the straps of my sweater to get rid of the chill I was feeling before slipping my hand into Tim's. I felt him gently squeeze our hands together as we walked hand in hand until we stood outside Mya's room.

I watched our daughter lying there sleeping, part of me feeling guilty for wanting to wake her.

When the nurse turned and saw us standing on the other side of the window, she came out of the room.

"Mr. and Mrs. Michaels?" the nurse acknowledged.

Tim squeezed my hand again.

"Before you can go in to be with Mya, Dr. Brooks would like to have a word with you. Do you know where his office is?"

"Yes," Tim replied, looking over at me and then back at the nurse.

My heart quickened. I grabbed the wall with my right hand to keep from falling. I didn't know what the doctor wanted to speak to us about, but of course, the worst had entered my mind.

Neither of us said a word as we turned and walked towards Dr. Brooks's office.

Tim knocked on the door, keeping his eyes on mine. When we heard the doctor speak, Tim turned the knob and opened the door.

I sat first, then Tim. Uneasy thoughts kept playing in my head. I tried to block them out, but failed miserably.

"We were told you needed to speak to us," Tim said.

"Yes, I do." Dr. Brooks shuffled a few folders around on his desk and picked one from the bottom. "Here we go," he mumbled more to himself. He opened the folder and began to speak, "All of Mya's vitals are looking good. In fact, she's put on a couple of ounces. I know that might not seem like much, but it'll take some time before she increases in weight." He looked at us, and then back down at the file. "Even with the respiratory distress, her lungs are developing as expected and showing signs that they are getting healthier and stronger. I'd like to say in another month or two, at the most, her lungs should be fully developed and we'll be able to remove the ventilator." He stopped, then looked up, focusing on me, then on Tim. "If she continues to grow—which all babies do—and her organs seem to be adapting, she'll be moved out of NICU. Although, we'd prefer her weight to be at least three pounds or more before we decide to move her. She still has a feeding tube, as you know, and we'll adjust the food intake each week. Eventually, she'll be able to be bottle-fed, and then we can start to remove more of the wires," Dr. Brooks nodded. "She's doing well, but..." he paused. "But, sometimes things happen so she's still at risk. We'll continue to monitor her. Remember when you go in to see her, your hands need to be washed and that you have on the required gowns and gloves. If you feel any sickness, I don't care if it's a runny nose or a small cough, please *do not* go in and see your baby. I know you've been told this, but I just want to make sure we're very clear on this!" he stated, firmly.

"Dr. Brooks?" I said, interrupting.

"Yes."

"Why are you telling us this? Did something happen while we weren't here?"

Dr. Brooks looked from me to Tim and back to me again. He cleared his throat, "One of the nurses caring for your daughter was feeling under the weather, though she was wearing the proper outfit, she still shouldn't have been in the room. I happened to be making my rounds when I entered the room; the nurse had a small cough. All of the staff members know *not* to do anything inside the rooms when they feel ill. They must step out, and then sterilize themselves before reentering," Dr. Brooks said.

"Has Mya caught a virus or something?" I asked, feeling nervous.

"I've been running blood-work on her, and so far— nothing, but I'll have to keep a close watch on her. The nurse said she had an itchy throat, nothing more, but I'm sorry, I cannot take that chance. I ran some blood-work on the nurse and the results were negative, but like I just said, I'd like to keep an eye on her just for a couple of days."

"Thank you, doctor. We appreciate you coming forth with this information," Tim said.

"It's part of my job, and I'm responsible for what goes on in this part of the hospital. You may go in and spend time with your baby, but please try not to stay for more than a half an hour at a time. She still needs plenty of rest for her body to grow and get stronger."

"Sure, we understand," Tim replied. "We appreciate what you're doing for her, and your concern to keep her safe and healthy. I'm sure it's what any doctor would do for their patient."

Dr. Brooks nodded in agreement.

"Is there anything else you would like to talk to us about?" I asked.

"No, but I'll keep you both posted, if something, anything, should occur. I can't say we're past the worst, but she is showing signs of getting stronger."

I nodded, reached for Tim's hand and squeezed it. We both stood and walked towards the door.

"Thank you, doctor for taking care of our daughter," I turned and said, before walking out the door.

We stood in front of Mya's room, helping each other with our gowns. Once the gloves and masks were on, we went inside. The nurse attending Mya handed her to me. I sat and held her for a while, then handed our baby to Tim, being careful not to interrupt the wires.

Through the mask, he gently placed his lips on Mya's forehead, giving her a gentle kiss. Mya opened her eyes, and her lips curved up into a slight smile.

I laughed and snuggled in close against Tim, "We're the luckiest parents in the world," I whispered.

He nodded in agreement and kissed my hair. When our time was up, we exited the room and discarded our gowns and gloves. As we walked to the elevator, Tim stopped and pulled me into his arms.

"I want to go see Samantha," I said. "Is she still in the hospital?"

"Yes, I think so. I'll walk you to her room."

The door to Samantha's room was cracked open when we arrived. I pushed the door wider and went inside.

Samantha was sitting up in her bed.

"Hey, Samantha, how are you doing?" I asked.

Samantha smiled, "Hi, Mrs. Michaels. I was just coloring a picture for you. Do you want to see it?" Samantha gleamed up at me.

"Yes, I'd love to see what you've drawn." I sat in the chair next to the bed as Samantha held up the picture for me to see.

"That's a beautiful picture you drew."

"Thank you. It's of you and me holding hands. I drew Mr. Michaels beside you holding your other hand," Samantha said, still smiling.

Tears surfaced in my eyes as I looked over the picture. I felt a slight pull on my heart.

"Do you like it?" Samantha asked, looking concerned.

"I love it. You did a wonderful job coloring it," I replied.

I wasn't sure what I should be feeling towards Samantha. I'd only known her since the start of second grade, but there was something there. Something inside my heart wanting to reach out and take her as my own, but was it right to be feeling this way about one of my students? Should I care so much about a child that wasn't mine? Of course, I could, but then there was Mya. She came first before anyone, but I couldn't help feeling the warmth inside me growing for Samantha. I knew without a doubt I would and could love them both.

Chapter 12

Before leaving the hospital, Tim and I spent another half an hour with Mya, and then he drove me home. Tim didn't want Ashley to have to drive out to the hospital if she didn't need to.

On the drive home, I brought up my thoughts about Samantha, "What do you think will happen with Samantha once she leaves the hospital?"

"Right now, I'm not sure what will happen. We haven't even gone to court yet. Even though we have enough evidence against her parents, we still don't know what the judge will decide. It will be up to the parents, unless of course, the judge fines them both at fault, and they lose all custody rights to the child. With what we have on the Berkley's, I don't see them getting any custody, but anything can happen," he replied.

"I always felt close to Samantha, like we have some kind of bond. I just pray that she doesn't have to go back into that house with them. I don't want them to continue to abuse her," I said, then turned and looked out the window.

"I agree with you there. I'm going to do everything I possibly can to keep that from happening," Tim assured me.

Inside, my heart swelled with love for Samantha. If I learned anything from my mother, it was that a woman's heart could love anyone unconditionally and still have room for more. *God I wished my mother were alive to see her first and only grandchild. How many years has it been now? Seven? Eight years?* My heart sank as I took in a deep breath and exhaled.

There wasn't a day that went by that I didn't think of my mother, but with all that had happened lately, my mind was exhausted. My father had left three years after I was born, which left my mother to raise me on her own. My mother never remarried, nor did she ever bring a man around the house. Sometimes I asked about my father, but my mother would always tell me, "He isn't worth talking or thinking about, and you shouldn't waste your time trying to find him. If he wanted you in his life he would have stayed." For the most part, she was right, but I couldn't help but wonder what he was like, and if there was a reason why he couldn't have stayed.

Once, I spent hours searching through my mother's room trying to find a photo of him, but had found nothing. I even went through the photo albums, but they only contained pictures of me. Some were taken of me and my mother, but mostly just me from birth until I married Tim. I sighed at the thought and felt Tim squeeze my hand.

"Is everything all right?" he asked.

I blinked, coming back to the present. "What was the question again?"

"You were in deep thought there for a moment. What were you thinking about?"

"My mother and Samantha. Just wishing she were here to see her grandchild is all."

Tim nodded and squeezed my hand again. "I'm sorry," he whispered. "I know you have a big heart, that's why you became a teacher. But Samantha will be in good hands with Michele Channels."

"Who's Michele Channels?"

"I've never mentioned her to you before?"

"I don't think so, at least I don't remember you mentioning her name," I replied.

"She's a foster parent. She takes care of five to six kids at a time until they get adopted or turn eighteen, but they usually only stay a few weeks to a couple of months, very few stay years."

"Where do they go?"

"They're adopted quickly or move to new homes, some in Illinois, but most move out of state."

"Oh."

"What was that for?"

"I was thinking that if Samantha got adopted from someone in another state, I wouldn't be able to see her again."

He said nothing, but I felt there was something he wasn't sharing with me. I rested my head back on the headrest and closed my eyes. I shouldn't be thinking about all of this. I needed to keep my thoughts only on Mya.

Tim pulled into the driveway and parked the car. I opened the door before Tim had a chance to come around to the passenger side. With everything going on, I had forgotten about the cesarean I had just had. I didn't have much pain, and when I did, something always took my focus off it.

He helped me out of the car and into the house. I made my way to the kitchen, retrieved a glass of water, took one of my pills, which I was surprised Tim had filled for me with what had happened last year, and set the empty cup in the sink. I decided I'd lie down for a while and get some much needed rest; besides, I knew Tim had to leave and go back to work anyway.

I climbed the stairs, letting Ashley know that we were home and that I was going to lie down for a while. In my room, I slipped out of my clothes, catching a glimpse of my body in the mirror. I glided my hand over the incision on the lower part of my abdomen. I couldn't believe it was just a few days ago that I was pregnant and had almost lost the baby.

The images of that day came rushing back. First, I was teaching the class, and then I was collecting the students' artwork. Even now, I was thankful that it happened after the children had left for the day. If I'd had stayed home, would I still be pregnant? I didn't think so. It wasn't like my job was strenuous and required me to lift heavy things or climb many stairs. In fact, I hadn't climbed any stairs. When I was pregnant I hadn't gained much weight, and by the looks of my body, I was still slim with a little belly bump.

I didn't tell Tim what my OB/GYN doctor had said about something being wrong with my uterus. It was at one of my visits without him. I hadn't told him because he would have probably started worrying about me, and made me stay home instead of teaching. *Was it my fault that I'd almost lost Mya?* I shook my head refusing to believe I'd been the cause of it. I recalled the doctor saying there was nothing he could do, but to monitor me until the baby was born.

I turned to view the side of my body in the mirror and saw Tim staring at me; his eyes shined as he smiled.

"Sorry," he said, his cheeks turning red from embarrassment.

"Sorry for what? You're my husband."

"It's been a while since… since you know?"

"Yes, it has. But I don't think we are allowed to have sex yet?"

"No, the doctor said at least six weeks or so, depending on how you feel."

"I think I've been over doing it lately, kind of tired today."

"Well, then let me help you into bed," he suggested.

I opened the top drawer of the dresser and grabbed one of Tim's old T-shirts, pulling it over my head. I peeled back the covers, climbed inside.

Tim pulled the blanket up and under my chin, then knelt down next to the bed. He gazed into my eyes and then kissed me on the lips. "I love you."

"I love you too, Tim." I closed my eyes and felt his lips touch my forehead as he kissed me goodbye and left the room.

Chapter 13

After waking from my much-needed nap, I dressed and went downstairs. My friend Ashley was sitting at the table when I entered the kitchen.

"Hey, Ash. What are you doing?" I asked, as I made my way to the table.

I saw her quickly wipe a hand across her cheek before I had a chance to stand beside her. Ashley swallowed and cleared her throat, "Oh, nothing. Was just sitting here thinking about my life and Lily," she quipped.

"Oh," I replied. "That's right you have a wedding coming up. I'm so sorry; I'd forgotten all about that."

"It's no problem. I honestly don't think there's going to be a wedding in my future," she whispered. "Remember earlier, I had told you that Rob and I hit a hard spot?"

I pulled out a chair and sat down across from my friend, "Yes, I remember, but I thought things were good with you and Rob."

Ashley took a deep breath, and then exhaled, "I just don't understand why relationships have to be so complicated. Things were fine between us and then..." Ashley paused. "And then, I don't know, he's just different now. Someone I know nothing about. But I don't want you to worry, I'll work it out when I get home," Ashley replied, trying to sound convincing.

"Are you sure? You know you can always talk to me. We've always had that kind of friendship. We're like two peas-in-a-pod," I smiled, giving my friend a nudge. Although there were some things I knew we didn't share. Some things were always kept hidden from our loved ones.

Ashley smiled back at me.

"Ash, are you sure you don't want to talk about what's bothering you?" I persisted. "I can tell this is really bothering you, but I won't push if you don't want to talk about it right now."

She lifted her head and gave a slim smile, "Thanks, Carla. I'm fortunate to have you as my friend," she replied.

"You mean best friend," I laughed.

Ashley joined in with a giggle.

"I'm really sorry I've been neglecting you since you've come to visit me," I noted.

Ashley reached out and touched my arm, "Forget about it. There's no reason for you to be sorry. I knew when I came out here that you had Mya. Besides, I needed some alone time anyway. Things have a way of just happening. Usually a sign to guide you in the right direction," she replied.

I nodded, "I guess you're right."

"I am," Ashley laughed.

I joined in, laughing along with my friend. It had been so long since I laughed this much; it felt good. "So, is there any place in particular you'd like to eat tonight?" I asked.

Ashley shrugged her shoulders, "Doesn't matter to me. You pick the place."

"How about the Brazilian restaurant, Chama Gaucha Steakhouse?"

"Sounds great!" Ashley said.

"Good! I'll call and get reservations and then once Tim gets home, we'll go to dinner."

Ashley grinned, and then said, "I'll head upstairs and freshen up before he gets home."

"Okay," I replied, as I watched my friend exit the kitchen. I could feel that something was terribly wrong with my friend, but I didn't want to push her to talk. Ashley would come to me when she was ready.

After making reservations for tonight's dinner, the phone rang in my hand. "Hello," I answered.

"Hey, hon," Tim replied. "Are we still going out to dinner tonight?"

"Yes, of course. Just waiting for you to get home."

"I just have to stop at the office, and then I'll be on my way."

"Sure, no problem. Is everything okay?"

"It couldn't be better!" he replied. "I'll be home soon."

Before I could reply, I heard a *click*, knowing that my husband had just hung up on me.

I set down the phone just as Ashley entered the room. She must have seen the perplexed look on my face and asked, "Is everything all right with you? With Mya?"

I looked at my friend, cleared my throat, "What? Yeah, everything's fine. That was Tim on the phone; said he'd be home soon, but then hung up without saying anything more. He didn't sound upset or anything, just anxious."

"I'm sure it's nothing," Ashley replied, waving a dismissive hand in the air. "He's been working hard on this case; he's probably just glad it's almost over."

"Yes, you're probably right. I don't need to be making something out of nothing, like I always do," I admitted.

Ashley walked over to me and threw an arm around my shoulder, "Come on, let's go sit outside until Tim gets home," she suggested. "We need some more girl time!"

"Okay," I replied, as I tried to shake the uneasy feeling in the pit of my stomach.

After slipping a sweater on, we made our way to the porch outside and sat down in the wooden chairs. I let out a long sigh as I lifted my legs and placed them on the footstool in front of me. "Haven't been pregnant for several days and my feet still hurt me," I announced.

"Trust me. You'll feel like yourself again soon. It takes time for your body to get back to the way it once was. Carrying a baby isn't an easy job, but I guess that's why we women get the pleasure of doing it?" Ashley stated. "Just be thankful you had her now and not…" Ashley slapped her hand to her mouth. "I'm sorry, I didn't mean for it to come out like that. I just meant…"

I raised my hand, "Don't worry about it. I know what you meant. Sometimes our mouths move faster than our brains. I would have loved to have carried Mya to full-term, but I guess I'm happy to have had her at all," I interjected.

"Yes, she's definitely a miracle baby," Ashley assured.

"Yes, she is," I nodded, then turned and looked out over the railing.

We sat in the chairs, talking and catching up on old times. My friend talked about some of the things she was going to do once she returned home and talked about her daughter Lily some more.

"I can't believe she'll be starting kindergarten this fall," I said. "I wish you'd brought her along with you. I haven't seen her in such a long time."

"I know, but with everything you have going on, I just didn't think it would've been a good idea," Ashley replied. "She would have been running around like crazy. I don't think the doctors would have let her in to see Mya, either.

I nodded, "Yeah, I guess you're right. Just miss seeing her, is all."

"Yeah, I miss her too, and I'm her mom," Ashley laughed.

A few minutes later, Tim arrived home. He said his hellos and went back inside to shower and change.

$$\sim \sim \sim \sim \sim$$

Sunday came faster than I expected. For some reason, I woke up early, unable to fall back to sleep. I couldn't believe how light it was outside at just five in the morning. I started the coffee pot and waited by the counter, eager to get the first cup.

Before the coffee maker sputtered to a finish, I quickly poured myself a cup and placed the pot back to finish brewing. I stirred in a couple teaspoons of sugars and sat down at the kitchen table.

I wasn't sure how long I'd sat there before Ashley entered the room.

"I hope I didn't wake you," I whispered.

"No, I was already up. I took a shower and packed my bag for the trip home today," Ashley replied as she walked to the coffee pot, poured a cup, and then sat across from me.

"I'm so going to miss you being here. I wish you could stay longer," I mumbled.

"I know, but I need to get back. Now that I've finished my classes early, I'm eager to start applying for an Architect job."

"Oh, that's right, you're graduating soon."

"Yep! Now, I can finally get my dream job, just like my father."

"I'm so happy for you. You seem to have everything you want," I said.

"Yeah, I suppose. Although I think I'll miss working at the Pediatrician's office. I loved helping out and being around all those babies and children, but it was nice while it lasted."

"I remember when I was young and had applied to a Nanny school in Cleveland, Ohio. I have always loved kids and wanted to have several of them myself, but I guess that's not in the cards for me."

"Oh, right. What made you become a teacher instead of a Nanny?"

"I guess I just had second thoughts and decided a teacher was more my calling," I replied.

"I can understand that. I actually was torn between the two careers, but I'm happy to be following in my father's footsteps, *God rest his soul*. He loved building things, and I loved working alongside him when he'd let me come with him," Ashley contested, taking a sip of her coffee.

I stood and walked to the refrigerator. "I'm going to make you a delicious breakfast so you don't have to stop and get something to eat on your way home."

Ashley smiled, "Thank you, Carla. Do you want any help?"

"No!" I protested. "You are my guest and besides, I love cooking. You just sit there and relax. You have a long drive ahead of you today."

She nodded in agreement.

After I finished frying the bacon, I started on the pancakes and whipping-up some eggs in a bowl.

Fifteen minutes later, I placed plates of cooked food on the table. I then took down two more plates from the cabinet and some silverware from the drawer.

Ashley stood and poured herself another cup of coffee and sat back down. She waited for me to sit before helping herself to the food.

After we ate, Ashley helped me clean up the dishes and prepare a plate for Tim, who was still sleeping on this early Sunday morning.

"Tell Tim I said goodbye and that it was nice seeing him again," Ashley said.

"I will, and you tell that pretty little girl of yours that I love her and can't wait to see her!"

We both went in for a hug and held each other tight; neither wanting to let go of the other.

I pulled slowly away and wiped the tears running down my face. I was going to miss my friend more than ever. I felt sad inside, wishing so much that Ashley could stay just a little longer, but knew she had to get back to her daughter and that we would see each other again soon. I would make sure of it.

Chapter 14

Weeks went by, and Mya, although she still had the wires and machines attached to her, seemed to be growing stronger. I wasn't certain when those would be removed.

Tim was busy with Samantha's case, and although I wasn't supposed to drive, there wasn't anything that could keep me away from driving to the hospital and being with my baby.

I had developed a routine each day I went to see her. I'd slip into a sterile gown and wash my hands before gently cradling Mya in my arms. I'd spend as much time with my daughter as the nurses allowed, and then went home.

But today—today was different when I arrived to see Mya. When I stopped in front of the glass window, Mya wasn't there. There wasn't a nurse in the room or even the incubator Mya had been in since she was born.

My heart began to pound hard, my breathing quickened. I turned from the window, looking frantically for anyone— someone who could tell me where my daughter was. Of course, only the worst entered my mind. *Had something happened to her? Did they move her to a different room and not tell me? Not call me?*

I spotted a nurse walking out of a room, ten maybe twenty feet away from me. I moved one foot in front of the other, even though they felt heavy as lead. I needed to stay positive and not think of the worst. *Easier said than done,* I thought.

I opened my mouth, but the words I'd tried to say seemed to be lodged deep in my throat. I tried again, and it sounded like a high chirp of a dying bird escaping from my dry throat. I needed to get ahold of myself.

Before I knew it, I was standing behind the nurse. I reached out and tapped the nurse's shoulder, "Excuse me, Miss. Can you tell me where Mya Michaels is? She's not in her room," I cried out, as I fought back the tears, wanting to escape.

The brunette nurse turned and was now facing me, "Didn't you get the call?" the nurse replied looking shocked.

"Call?" I whispered, and then my voice slightly rose as I continued to speak. "What call? I didn't get a call!"

I started to panic, my heart beating faster and faster. My hand trembled as I touched my lips. Tears I tried hard to hold back began to slide down my face. "What's happened to my daughter? Did something happen to her?"

I started to come unraveled. Questions came pouring out of me. Questions I just wanted answers to. Why wasn't the woman giving me any answers? However, I wasn't even giving the nurse time to answer them, was I?

"Come sit and I'll..."

I cut her off, "No! Just tell me what happened to her? Where is she?" I began to cry harder.

"She's in surgery. I'm afraid her heart stopped," the nurse said as she touched my arm.

I sucked in a breath and then another and another. I instantly became light-headed from all the breaths I'd taken in. The nurse put her hands on my arms and guided me to a chair by the wall.

"It helps if you put your head between your legs," the nurse suggested.

I did as I was told and stayed in the bent position until I felt the faintness slowly disappear. I straightened and wiped the wetness from my cheeks, "What do you mean her heart stopped? Is she…?" I paused. I didn't want to say the word; didn't even want to think it!

"No," the nurse replied quickly, hoping to comfort me.

I swallowed and looked over at her. The nametag on her scrubs, read *Beth*. "Do you know what happened, Beth?"

"Just that her heart stopped, and Dr. Brooks immediately took her into surgery."

"When did this happen?"

"Couple of hours ago," she replied.

"And you said someone called us?"

"I did," Beth stated. "I called and left a message on both numbers that were listed on the computer."

I'd seen Beth many times coming here to see my daughter, though we'd never been introduced to one another, I still knew who she was. I, of course, didn't want to think the worst. *But,* the truth was, I didn't know what was actually happening to Mya. Mya was in surgery; she'd been there for the past two hours, and with this kind of surgery, Beth had said, she could be there for many more hours—maybe all day.

I racked my brain on what I was doing two hours ago. I'd woken up, had coffee, something to eat, and then took a shower before leaving the house to come straight here. *It could be possible they called while I was in the shower this morning,* I thought. I didn't live but ten minutes from the hospital so there was no way I'd missed the call driving here.

"As soon as I hear something, I'll give you a call," Beth promised.

"No!" I said a little too loud. "I'm not going anywhere. I'm staying right here until I know she is fine and back in her room."

Beth nodded.

"I have to call my husband," I stressed. "I have to tell him what has happened. He needs to be here!" I stood and walked down the hall towards the waiting room.

Chapter 15

I clenched the cell phone in my hand that was pressed against my ear. I had scrolled through my contacts, and now I waited for Tim to answer.

I hadn't said anything to Tim about working all those long hours. I occupied my time by coming to the hospital. I wasn't sure just how many trips a day I'd made in these past couple of weeks when I should've been resting. Without Tim at home, I didn't want to sit alone in the house. I hated being alone. It frightened me. What would I ever do without him by my side? Someone that loved me more than life! I hoped I'd never have to find out what life would be without Tim.

His voice echoed in my ear as I listened once again to his voicemail. "Tim, it's Carla. Mya's in surgery! You have to come to the hospital as soon as possible!" I wailed, as the words raced out of me. I took in a long breath, exhaled, "I arrived at the hospital a little while ago and Mya wasn't in her room. When I finally spoke to a nurse, Nurse Beth, she said that Mya was taken into surgery two hours ago. Tim, Mya's heart stopped! Please say you'll come to the hospital?"

I wasn't sure why I'd asked a question when I was leaving a message on his phone for him. It's not like he'd be able to answer. I hit the end button and continued to pace the small room, replaying the words Nurse Beth had told me. *Their Mya was in surgery. Her heart stopped.* That was all I kept thinking about.

I went through the motions of grabbing a cup and filling it with coffee as if I was comatose. I had to keep myself busy.

I glanced at my watch for what seemed like the tenth time, or was it more? It had been six hours since Mya was taken into surgery. *How much longer were the doctors going to be?* I wasn't sure about that either. I wasn't sure about a lot of things lately. I should've been here with my daughter, and then maybe she'd be lying in her small portable bed right this minute. Like I believed my being here would've kept Mya's heart from stopping.

Unthinkable thoughts entered my mind. *If*—NO! *When, Mya gets out of surgery. I couldn't think that Mya wouldn't make it, wouldn't survive. She had too! She just had to—live!*

I made one more lap around the waiting room, and then sat down. The second I placed my head in my hands, I heard a woman's voice speak to me.

"Is everything all right, dear?" the kind old lady asked.

I looked up and shook my head, but not in a *no, I'm not fine* way. Not that I was fine, but in a way it helped to clear the thoughts from my head. This woman looked vaguely familiar. Almost like my mother, but I knew that wasn't possible—she was dead.

"Sorry?" I asked, confused by the woman's kind gesture, as I looked her over. The room seemed to get brighter since she'd arrived, almost as if I were dreaming the whole experience.

"I see that you are sad about something, my sweet child," the kind old woman replied.

I sucked in a breath. There was only one person in my life that had referred to me by that name. I didn't know if I should answer the woman. She was a stranger to me, wasn't she? How could the woman know why I was sad? The old lady just wanted to comfort me, that's all she wanted to do, but still as I sat in the chair, I replayed the words over in my head, *my sweet child.*

I motioned the woman to the chair next to me. "My baby girl. She's only a month old and…" I blinked several times, allowing the tears to flow down my face. "And the nurse said that her heart stopped, that she's in surgery and could be there for a while."

The woman placed her hand on mine, giving it a gentle squeeze. I sat still, watching as the woman did this, but I couldn't feel her touch. I'd seen her touch me and squeeze my hand, but nothing.

I had felt nothing.

"There, there, now, my sweet child. Things don't always seem as they are. It will be hard at first, but you'll work through them. Your daughter will live on, and so will your husband, Tim," the woman whispered in a sweet and caring voice, just as my mother used to do.

Wait! I thought. *How did she know my husband's name was Tim? I hadn't said his name. I didn't mention him at all! And what did she mean that my daughter will live on and so will Tim? She can't mean... No! There're both fine! There're both alive and well!* My mind screamed in fear!

But Tim hadn't answered his phone. I hadn't talked to him since early this morning. He didn't know about Mya yet. I had to be dreaming this. Tim was alive and well! He had to be!

"How do you know, Tim?" I asked.

The woman smiled and patted my hand, again. Still seeing her do this, but not feeling it. "I must go, but remember what I said. It won't always be this hard. Follow your heart, and it will lead you to the very thing you've been wanting, my dear sweet child."

I glanced down at my hands, then back up. The woman was gone. I jolted from the chair and ran to the doorway. I looked down both ends of the corridor, but saw no one.

Was I losing my mind? Did I imagine the whole thing? Yes, I had! I had to have been dreaming because only my mother had ever called me, "sweet child", and she was dead!

$$\sim \ \sim \ \sim \ \sim \ \sim$$

I shook my head again, trying to erase from my mind what had just happened. I was losing it and seeing my dead mother in the process. There was no other reason for what I had just witnessed. It had to be from sitting in this room since I'd arrived this morning.

I walked over to the corner table against the wall, where two coffee dispensers sat. I was about to have my fourth cup of coffee and nibble on a muffin that had been sitting there since I'd arrived this morning.

I took a bite and spit it back into my hand. It was stale and tossed it in the garbage can next to the table.

I sat back down in the same chair, placing my cup on the table next to me. I nearly spilled my coffee when I saw Dr. Brooks enter the room. I was on my feet and walking towards him before he had a chance to acknowledge me first.

With trembling hands, I crossed my arms against my chest as if I were hugging myself.

"Mrs. Michaels," he began. "Is Mr. Michaels here with you?"

"No," I whispered, shaking my head. "I called him this morning, but he hasn't called me back."

"Come, let's have a seat over here while we talk," he suggested. He rolled his shoulders back and made his way to the chair.

I hesitated, then followed, sitting down next to him. "Is Mya okay?" I whispered, my eyes searching his.

I continued to watch as Dr. Brooks lifted his head and cleared his throat, "I'm so sorry, Mrs. Michaels. We did everything we could to save her, but she was just too small, too weak."

As the words registered in my head, then my heart, I slid from the chair to my knees and began to rock back and forth. "No, no, no!" I pleaded. "She can't be dead! She just can't be!" I began to sob uncontrollably, as I gulped in breaths, choking and sobbing harder and harder.

"I'm so sorry to have to tell you this without your husband here with you." He placed his hand on my shoulder and gave a slight squeeze. "Mrs. Michaels is there someone I can call? Someone that can stay with you?" he whispered.

I didn't answer right away. "If I can't reach Tim, I'll try calling my friend Veronica," I said between sobs.

"If you'd like, I could ask one of the nurses to stay with you until someone shows up," he offered.

I nodded and cried as I continued to rock on my knees.

Dr. Brooks left the room and returned with Nurse Beth at his side. They stood in the doorway whispering, before Beth came to my side. She knelt down to the floor and helped me to sit in the chair next to her. Beth comforted me while I continued to mourn.

"Would you like for me to call someone?" Beth asked, finally.

I nodded and reached for my purse on the floor. I pulled out my phone, hit the home key, and saw that there were still no messages from Tim. I unlocked the screen and opened my contacts folder. After searching and finding Veronica's name, I handed it to Beth. I couldn't find it in myself to tell my friend that Mya died. I didn't even want to think about it.

Beth stood, walked to the doorway and into the hall. I wasn't able to hear the whole conversation between them, but listened anyway to what I could hear.

"Hi, Veronica, this is Beth Melton, I work at Silver Cross Hospital. I'm sorry to be the one to call you, but Carla really needs you to come to the hospital. I'm afraid Mya has passed away," Beth spoke in a hushed whisper.

There was silence for a moment.

"Veronica, can you try and get a hold of Tim for her? Carla said she's tried a few times and he's not picking up."

Then there was silence.

Part Two

<u>Thinking of you</u>

There is a smile

Upon my face

Whilst I think of you.

Thoughts of you dance

Forever

Through my mind.

By: S. M. Hampton

Chapter 16

A month had passed since Tim and Mya were buried in Overlook Cemetery, a few miles from our house. I don't think I could ever call it my house; it'll always be ours. It was a home Tim and I built together as a couple. A home that made us a family.

The newspapers stated that Tim Michaels, along with his colleague Pat Atkins, were at the courthouse when the incident occurred. Judge Henry Cole had just given his final judgment, when the commotion started. Two shots were fired. An Officer of the court was injured and Tim who hadn't had time to take cover was shot in the chest, dying instantly.

With the help of my friends Ashley, Veronica, and Pat Atkins, I was able to attend Tim and Mya's funeral without becoming overly hysterical. Since the funerals, I hadn't found much effort to climb out of bed and live my life.

What life?

I argued with myself endless times. *My husband was dead! My daughter had died!* I didn't see a reason to continue without them. Why should I? I had nothing! Nothing to come home to. No one to love me like Tim did.

I'd felt guilty for leaving things unresolved with Tim before his sudden death. We had only been able to attend one meeting with a marriage counselor, which I'd told my friend Alexis on the phone before the funerals. I still hadn't meant for him to hear my words about being so unhappy. I never really meant to say them, but what good does it do now to continue to feel guilty about something I couldn't fix—couldn't take back?

I also had thoughts to be with him. Swallow a whole bottle of pills to kill myself, but then what if I didn't end up with him, but in another place unlike the heaven we hear about?

I hadn't even been the one to call Alexis or Ashley when Tim died. My two best friends in the world, and I couldn't find it in myself to call them, to tell them what had happened. I didn't want to talk to anyone, about anything. I just wanted to curl up in my bed and just be forgotten!

It was my friend Veronica, who had made the calls and told them what had happened. Alexis wasn't able to attend the funeral because of her treatments with her breast cancer, which I'd found out the night before my daughter and husband had died. Ashley came alone, not wanting to cause me any more grief, bringing Lily with her.

I rolled over and slowly opened my swollen crusted eyes. Light poured in, blinding me instantly, and I quickly squeezed them shut, again.

I breathed out a long weighted sigh. I hadn't brushed my teeth in days, and tasted the pungent layer of plaque on my tongue and teeth. I swallowed, breathed out another breath, and slowly climbed out from under the blankets.

I gazed around the room; clothes lined the floor around me as I placed my foot down to stand up. Tim's clothes that I'd taken from his dresser and from his closet were scattered around the room. I even had some of his things in bed with me.

The wooden floor under my bare feet creaked with every step I took. Once inside the bathroom, I used and flushed the toilet, then stood in front of the mirror. How long had it been since I took a shower? I couldn't remember. An odor lingered off my unwashed skin. My oily and unwashed hair was sticking up on one side and looked as if a mouse had made a home.

I peeled off my clothes and turned the water on in the shower. I climbed inside and let the hot steamy water run over my thin-boned body. I'd lost too much weight from not eating these past few weeks. It was only when my friend Veronica came over that I pretended to eat. After she'd leave, I would crawl back under the covers and hibernate until she showed up at the house, again.

After shampooing, washing, and rinsing, I turned off the water, grabbed a clean towel from the hook, and dried off my body. I stepped out, wrapped the towel around my head, then slipped into my robe, and walked back into the bedroom. My eyes scanned the room, uncertain what to do next.

I stepped over the piles of clothes as I made my way to a dresser against the wall. After slipping on some clean clothes, I turned and sighed. I knew I had to pull myself together. I had to start over, alone. Something I wasn't sure

I could handle. Now that Tim and Mya were both gone, I had no one. No family that I really knew of. I wasn't even sure if my father was still alive. If he was still out there somewhere. Did I really even care? *No! Not really!*

I bent over, scooped up a handful of Tim's clothes, and set them on the bed. I did this, until the floor was clean. I sat down next to the pile, grabbed one of his shirts and placed it under my nose. I inhaled, smelling his scent. Although it wasn't as strong as it was days, or maybe weeks ago, but I could still make out the faint smell of his cologne.

I smelled each and every shirt, and then folded it, putting them into a neat pile. When I finished, I walked downstairs and into the garage, grabbing several flattened cardboard boxes we had kept since we moved in the house ten years ago and went back upstairs.

Thirty minutes later, I had stacked all of the boxes filled with Tim's clothes into a corner in the bedroom. Now, all I had to do was take them to Goodwill. Shaking the thought from my head, I turned and went downstairs and into the kitchen, pouring myself a cup of cold stale coffee. I was in no rush to get rid of his things.

I turned, opened the microwave, placed the cup inside and pressed two-minutes. I leaned against the counter, my eyes scanning the room. I saw that the answering machine was blinking and strolled over to play the message.

"Hey, Carla, it's Veronica. I'll be over later after work," she informed me.

I could tell that my friend's voice was distraught. I really couldn't blame her for feeling that way. Veronica came over every couple of days after work and even on weekends. She sat with me. Even though, I wouldn't participate in the conversations, she'd continue to talk to me, until she decided to go home. I felt my heart warm with emotions for my friend who gave up so much of her time to be with me. I wasn't even sure why I decided today was the day that I'd start *trying* to live again.

I snapped out of my thoughts when I heard another voice on the machine.

"Carla, it's Pat. I know this is a bad time, but I need you to come into the office as soon as you're able to. I've gone through a few of Tim's things here, but I need you to help sort through some things I don't know what to do with. Call me when you get this," Pat said.

The machine beeped, indicating there were no more messages. I grabbed my coffee from the microwave, shuffled past the phone on the wall, and opened the door to the backyard. The sun was out and the air felt warm as I sat down on the swing at the end of the porch. Tears rolled down my face.

Chapter 17

I sat outside for a couple of hours, trying to *will* myself to drive to Tim's office. I wasn't sure if I could. It was hard enough this morning that I'd put all of Tim's things in boxes. Now, Pat wanted me to pack up his things at the office too? I wasn't so sure I could do that. I didn't want to think about moving forward. I didn't want to think about not having Tim here—period!

I wiped away the tears that continued to slide down my face. I needed to do this. I had to do this. I blew out a single breath. "No Mya. No Tim," I mumbled into the air around me. I had been doing that a lot lately.

I stood, walked into the house and up the stairs. I *flicked* on the light in the bathroom, brushed my hair, and pulled it into a ponytail. I would at least try to drive to his office, if anything I did need to get out of the house and into civilization—again.

~ ~ ~ ~ ~

I parked the car and turned off the ignition. I was sitting in the parking lot. Now all I had to do was open the door and walk inside.

I placed my hand on the handle.

The door opened.

Then I slammed the door shut! Still sitting inside. I just wasn't sure whether I could go through with this right now. Maybe it was too soon?

I shook my head in disgust, took in a deep breath, filling up my lungs and exhaled. I needed to make a decision to either get out of the car or drive back home.

Next thing I knew, I was standing outside the car, taking tiny motionless steps towards the building Tim's office was in. When I reached the door, I swallowed, turned the knob, and pulled it open. I took a hesitant step inside, slowly moving forward. I stopped, sweat rolling down the back of my neck.

I couldn't remember the last time I'd been in his office. Actually, yes, I could. It was right after he'd leased the building. There hadn't been any furniture yet when I was here.

I looked around the room, as if seeing it for the first time. A small oak desk sat in front of me, covered with manila folders. A printer was along the wall to the right of the desk. Filing cabinets covered the back wall. I looked to my left and saw several chairs and a small coffee table for the clients. Against the wall on my right, was a table with a K-cup machine and condiments.

I heard noise coming from a room down the hall. I walked around the oak desk, making my way to the door. Pat sat behind the desk with his head in his hands.

The last time I'd seen him was at the funeral. His blond hair was longer now, past his ears. *Has he been struggling with the loss of Tim too?* I hadn't thought about what others were going through. Another selfish act of mine. Always thinking I had it worse than others. Pat worked with Tim eight to ten hours a day, and even more when they had a case to work on. I cleared my throat, not wanting to startle him.

Pat quickly looked up, pushing his chair back. "Hey, Carla. You made it," Pat whispered.

I forced a smile and nodded.

Pat walked around the desk, also piled high with manila folders, and gave me a long needed hug.

"How are you doing?" he asked as he pulled away.

I gave another small smile and shrugged my shoulders, "As good as anyone can be, I guess."

He nodded. "Well, I've been going through his open court cases that I'll be taking over. Since we *were* partners and all; just trying to get things organized."

I looked around the room. "Tim had all these cases?" I hadn't realized how busy he'd been. Now, I knew why he was at the office late most nights.

"Most of them, yes. Some cases have more than one folder—it's put in a different folder once it's closed out and placed in a filing cabinet. These past few months we haven't had anything filed away because our secretary…ah, well…she had to take a leave of absence before we were able to get a replacement for her. So, things have gotten a little unorganized," he elaborated.

"Unorganized? Really?" I glanced around the room. *Tim was never unorganized,* I smiled at the memory. "Well, where do you want me to start?"

I walked over to a hook on the wall and hung up my purse and sweater.

"Start?" Pat questioned.

"Yes, you look like you could use some help," I said.

"Yeah, I do, but…" Pat paused. "I can't ask you to help me. I didn't ask you here to work…"

I interrupted, not giving him a chance to finish what he wanted to say. "You didn't ask me—I *want* to help you get things re-organized," I stated. *Maybe it would keep my mind off of Tim and Mya for a while.* "So where do I start?"

"Well, okay, if you're sure you want to. I do appreciate your wanting to help," he gave a weak smile. "You can start over there," Pat pointed at the pile on the floor. "Most are in alphabetical order. They just need filed away in the cabinet over there."

I nodded, letting him know I understood. Besides it wasn't like I had anything else to do, and looking around the room I could see that Pat could use some help.

~ ~ ~ ~ ~

Hours later, I had the floor cleared of folders and was helping Pat with the ones on the desk. A few were open cases, but more than half needed a quick glance through and then could be filed away.

My attention was drawn to look at the file in my hand, my eyes scanning over the name on the folder, *Samantha Berkley*. I was holding the last case Tim had been working on. The one that got him *accidentally* killed.

I hadn't seen Samantha since Mya was alive, hadn't even thought about her. Heck, I hadn't even considered when I'd go back to work, teaching the children that at one time fulfilled my life.

I ran my finger over the letters of Samantha's name, and then quickly looked over at Pat. I turned towards the filing cabinet, pretending to file it, and slid the folder in a box that contained Tim's belongings from the office that I'd be taking home with me.

Chapter 18

I arrived home just before dark and carried the box from Tim's office into the house. I placed it on the kitchen table and went back to the car for the groceries I'd picked up on the way home. Before leaving Tim's, no now Pat's office, I had asked Pat to let Veronica know that she didn't need to come over tonight like she had planned.

Within record time, I'd put away all the groceries and stood at the dinette table, emptying the box. My mind was unsure of what to do, though I'd known the moment I held the file in my hands at the office what my intentions would be. I *wanted* to, no, I *needed* to read the file Tim had on Samantha Berkley. She was my student. A child who was abused by her own parents. End of story!

I pulled the chair out from the table and sat down. I graciously smoothed my hand over the folder, took in a deep breath, and opened the file.

There were several pictures of Samantha clipped to the inside cover. I released the paperclip and gathered them in my hand. The first picture of Samantha showed no signs of abuse. In fact, I knew the picture well, as it was the exact photo taken at the beginning of the school year. The same picture that was used on the school website where I and other teachers posted the student's grades each week.

I moved to the next one and gasped at the horror of what Samantha's parents had done to her. I flashed back to when I'd seen Samantha in the hospital, two months ago. She hadn't looked as bad as the photo made her look. She had bruises, of course, but for some reason the photo had brought the colors out.

I moved on to the next picture and the next, until I had seen every part of Samantha's body that was covered in painful colors. A tear rolled down my face and dropped off my chin. I didn't even have the strength to wipe it away—I didn't care. I'd been crying for a month; what was another tear?

Setting the photos aside, I started reading Tim's words. He noted that he had a copy of the interview on a recorder. I looked at all the items on the table that I'd taken out of the box and saw a small recorder to the right of me. I grabbed it, turned it on, and hit the play button:

> **"February 18th, 2015, at 10:01 a.m., nothing on this recording has been edited or altered in anyway,"** the voice was Pat Atkins.

> **"My name is Pat Atkins, and I'm here with my associate, Tim Michaels. We are at Silver Cross Hospital to ask Samantha Berkley questions**

about what occurred at her home on the evening of February 17th, 2015. Samantha Berkley, I want you to know that I'll be recording everything we talk about."

"Will my mommy and daddy hear what I say? They'll be really, really mad at me, if they find out. I don't want them to find out," Samantha Berkley whispered.

"Not if you don't want them to," Tim's voice stated on the recorder.

I gasped at the sound of my husband's voice. Hearing it made me miss him even more. I sat up straight in the chair, holding my head high. No! I had to do this! I had to hold it together at least until I was done listening to the recorded conversation.

Pat Atkins's voice filled the air, "Before Tim Michaels begins asking you questions, can you please state your name for the record?"

"My name is Samantha Marie Berkley."

"How were things when you left for school yesterday morning?" I heard Tim ask Samantha.

"Okay, I guess."

"Were your mommy and daddy upset with you before you left for school?"

"No. They're not around in the morning when I leave for school."

"What do you mean they're not around? Do they both work or something?" I heard Pat Atkins ask Samantha.

"No, my mommy doesn't work. I think they're still sleeping, but I don't know for sure. I'm not allowed to go in their bedroom."

"Who gets you up for school?" Tim's voice resumed questioning.

"I do." I heard Samantha quip.

"So, you're telling us that you're the one that gets yourself up in the morning?" It was Tim asking again.

"Yes, sir."

"You don't have to call me, "sir"; Tim will be fine."

"But my daddy said I should always use my manners. I'll

get in trouble if I don't use my manners. My daddy *don't* like ungrateful children."

There was a long pause.

"What about breakfast?" Tim asked.

"I make myself a bowl of cereal, if there's a box of cereal in the house."

"Do you buy your lunch at school?"

"No. Don't tell my mommy," Samantha's voice fell to a whisper, "I hide a paper bag in my backpack and—"

"And what?" Tim asked.

"If I keep very quiet," the child whispered again, "I go through the kitchen looking behind all the cabinet doors for food that my mommy hides from me."

"How do you know your mommy hides food from you?" Tim whispered.

"She told me so!"

I was shocked by Samantha's outburst!

"What does she say to you?" Pat Atkins chimed in.

"She said to me that if I touch what isn't mine, she'd make sure I never touch anything ever again."

"Is that what happened last night? Is that why you have a cast on your arm?" It was Tim asking the question.

"I know I shouldn't have, but I forgot when I got home."

"What did you forget?"

I started to tear up at my husband's concerned tone. I leaned in real close to listen to her response.

"You can tell us, sweetie."

"At school we did this art project the day Mrs. Michaels was there..."

I was surprised when Samantha referred to me. My heart warmed, but at the same time, I was sad because I missed her.

"Mrs. Michaels said she loved what I drew and asked if she could hang it up for everyone to see. I was so excited because she was so proud of me. I like making her proud of me. She's a really nice teacher, Mrs. Michaels."

I smiled at what Samantha had said. I could visualize the toothless grin on her face, without even seeing her.

"I wish I could have her for all of my classes. I was so excited that I ran all the way home, instead of taking the bus to tell my mommy and daddy. When I swung open the door, it hit the table against the wall and a vase fell to the floor. I tried to clean it up before my mommy noticed, but... but the noise must have *woked* her up because she ran out of the bedroom like her hair was on fire or something."

"And then what happened?" Pat Atkins asked the question.

"She looked down at the floor and saw me trying to clean up the mess I had made. Before I could slip from her reach, she grabbed me by my hair, and that's when I tripped over something and fell and hit the fireplace. I was trying to tell her that my arm hurt, but I don't think she heard me with all the yelling she was doing. My arm hurt really bad, I started crying, and… and she grabbed me."

"What happened next?" Pat's voice continued.

Tim interrupted, "Go ahead, it's okay, you can tell us."

The sound of Samantha's sniffles filled the room. "I must have dropped the envelope from my bag that Mrs. Michaels had given me before I left school the other day. I was supposed to give it to my mommy and daddy, but I was afraid they would get mad at me and punish me again. My mommy picked it up and was holding it. She didn't even open it up. She just started screaming at me. She grabbed my hair again and dragged me to my room." I could hear Samantha crying as she spoke.

"I remember my head hitting the floor when she let go of me, and I started crying harder. My head hurt really bad, and my arm hurt too. I think she just wanted me to stop crying." Samantha sniffled into the recorder.

"I tried to, I really tried, but I couldn't stop. Then my daddy came in and started screaming at me because he was saying I was being too loud. I don't like it when my daddy gets mad."

"What did your daddy do, Samantha?" I heard the anger in Tim's voice.

"His foot hit my side. He must have had his big work boots on because it hurt more than the other times he kicked me."

"Go on." Tim said encouragingly, but I could still hear his disgust.

"I heard pounding on our front door. My daddy stopped and left the room. So, I crawled as quickly as I could under the bed away from them."

"Is that when the policemen showed up?" Pat asked.

I could tell Pat was upset as well. This is horrible, I thought to myself.

"I remember a man with a gun on his belt. He told me I had to come out from under the bed and to keep my eyes open, that I couldn't sleep. I *got* to be wheeled out on some kind of bed with wheels, and they put me in a truck with loud sirens and flashing lights. I don't know what happened to my mommy and daddy because I didn't see them when I was taken outside."

"Okay, I think that's enough for today." Tim's voice ended the ordeal.

~ ~ ~ ~ ~

Silence filled the air as I wiped the tears that streamed down my face. I reached for a napkin on the far side of the table, blew my nose, then quickly stood and ran to the sink to vomit. Never in my life had I ever listened to a case that Tim had worked on. Even if I had, this case was different. This case was about one of my students. A student I was fond of! *But,* more than anything, hearing the conversation… sickened me.

I grabbed a glass from the cabinet beside me and filled it with tap water. I took slow sips, hoping it would stay down.

There was no way I'd be able to finish going through the file tonight. No! I'd wait until tomorrow to continue. What I'd heard just minutes ago would give me enough nightmares for the rest of my life.

Chapter 19

The following morning, the conversation was still fresh in my mind, and part of me wished I hadn't listened to it in the first place.

I poured another cup of coffee, walked back to the table, and grabbed the file I had started reading last night. I decided to wait a day or so, before reading more about Samantha. The words coming from the recorder still spun violently in my head.

I skimmed the items that remained on the table. I spotted a yellow envelope with Tim's office address on it and picked it up. I flipped it over, noticing that it was still sealed. *Had he received this in the mail and didn't get the chance to open it?* I flipped it back over to confirm the date. It had been delivered exactly four weeks ago.

I sat down in the chair, forced my index finger under the flap and slowly inched it along the edge, careful not to get a paper cut. Once I finished, I slipped my hand inside and pulled out several papers. I set the envelope on the table and scanned over the papers in my hand. Starting with the first sheet, I began to read:

March 9th, 2015

Dear Tim Michaels,

Enclosed you will find 3 out of 4 results for the DNA test you have requested. I will be waiting for the remaining samples to determine the results. Again, these test are 99.99% accurate.

If you have any questions, please feel free to call our office with the number provided below.

Sincerely,
Mrs. Barbara Collins
Genetic DNA Laboratories, Inc.
1-700-555-5555

I wasn't exactly sure what I was about to read. *DNA? Why would he be doing a DNA test?* My mind was already jumping to conclusions, and I hadn't even read the remaining pages. Why did I assume it was about Tim in the first place? *It could be for some other case he was working on,* I contested.

I flipped the sheet of paper over and placed it facedown on the table. The next page had random numbers on it. I scanned down the paper, saw Martha Ann Berkley, and under her name Samantha Marie Berkley.

I couldn't think why Tim would have to do a DNA test on them. I read the numbers between the mother, child, and father.

The numbers indicated for the father didn't match the child's, but the mother had some similarities. I wasn't sure what the numbers and percentages meant. I placed the paper facedown on the other sheet and moved to the next page of the report.

Combined Paternity Index – 36,590 to 1 Probability of Paternity – 0%

Conclusion:

The alleged father, John Berkley, is excluded as the biological father of Samantha Marie Berkley. Based on the genetic testing results, the probability of paternity is 0% when compared to an untested random man of the North American population. (Prior Probability – 0.5) At least 99.99% of the North American population is excluded from the possibility of being the biological father of the child.

The paragraph stated that John Henry Berkley **was excluded** *from being* the father of Samantha Marie Berkley. *Had he adopted her? On the other hand, did Martha claim that he was the father of her unborn baby eight years ago? Or, had she herself not known that he wasn't the real father?* I thought as the questions swirled around in my head.

None of what I read made much sense. I had no clue why Tim had the procedure done in the first place. It could have been something they did with every case. How would I know for sure unless I asked Pat about it? No, I didn't need him finding out that I had taken a file that was not legally mine to take.

I flipped the sheet of paper over, placing it on the table. My eyes glanced at the last sheet in my hand. I sucked in a quick breath. "What would… Why would…" I couldn't finish the words that fumbled out of my mouth. My brain was frozen solid. I couldn't think; I couldn't even breathe.

I shut my eyes, took in a deep breath, held it, and then let it out. I opened my eyes, but nothing was different from before. Tim's name was still on the last paper I held in my hands.

Chapter 20

I slowly read over the paper, just like I did with the others. *But,* when I got to the end, there were no numbers. Nothing that indicated he was Samantha's father. *And nothing to indicate that he wasn't,* my brain quickly noted.

I shook my head, trying to shake the thoughts from my mind. I didn't want to believe that he had a DNA test to show if he was Samantha's father. Then it hit me, because then it would mean that he'd had an affair.

"NO!" My mind screamed. I was not going to let myself think such crap! Tim wouldn't do that to me. Would he? He had been spending a lot of time at the office, so I thought.

"No, no, no!" I shouted into the empty room. I gathered up the papers and quickly shoved them back into the yellow envelope and tossed it into the box. I wasn't going to sit here and think about what I'd just read.

After a few silent minutes, I looked down at the table in front of me and saw Samantha's class picture. I reached out my hand and slid the photo towards me. I looked at every detail of my student and found only one thing that resembled my husband. Their eye color was the same, but that didn't mean anything. There was nothing that told me they were father and daughter! It wasn't like the color blue was a rare eye color.

I couldn't do this anymore. I pushed back the chair, making the wooden legs scrap across the floor. The high-pitched sound echoed through the deserted room. As I shoved the chair back to its spot under the table, the force I gave it made the chair tip over and fall to the floor, which in turn made me jump. I sucked in a deep breath, telling myself to relax. I was over-reacting, needed to chill-out, think everything through, and not jump to conclusions. I bent over, picked up the chair, and with little effort, eased the chair back to its original spot.

I grabbed my coffee cup from the table and walked to the counter. After pouring myself a fresh cup, I held the hot mug between my hands and paced the kitchen. Unanswered questions rolled around in my head.

We had been married for ten years now, but it was as if I hadn't really known my husband. Not really! I thought we talked about everything; told each other our deepest secrets. Our dreams and sexual fantasies, even. It was hard for me to believe he'd cheat on me, to have sex with anyone but me.

My mind immediately went back to the DNA test. *Then why would he have taken the test?* I didn't know the answer to that question. Then I remembered what the letter had said: `I will be waiting for the remaining samples to determine the results.`

I stopped in my tracks. *Why had he omitted his samples to be tested!* It was as if a light bulb had turned on above me. If I wanted the truth, I had to search for samples of Tim and send them in. One small question nagged at me. *Why hadn't he done that to begin with?* If anyone were to take such a test, wouldn't they gather everything at one time and send it in? The answer to that would have to go unanswered too. There was no way of asking him now.

I walked to the table, took out the envelope and reached inside for the papers. I read over the letter and spotted an address at the bottom of the page. Now, all I had to do was open the boxes upstairs and search all of Tim's belongings.

~ ~ ~ ~ ~

An hour later, I sat hunched on my knees, digging in the last box. I'd gone through each and every one and found nothing. *Had I even packed his hairbrush?* Probably not, since I was planning to donate his things to Goodwill.

I closed the flap on the box and sat back on my heels. When the answer finally came to me, I quickly ran into the bathroom. I stood inside the room, rummaging through the cabinets and the drawers. I couldn't remember where I'd placed his hairbrush. I looked down at the obvious place. Right where I'd put them, in the wastebasket.

Back downstairs, I went into the office and grabbed a bubble wrapped envelope. Returning once more to the kitchen, I proceeded to copy the address, placing the items inside. I also wrote a quick note to this Barbara woman, letting her know what was in the envelope, and to send the results to my home address, which I had also written on the letter.

I glanced at the clock on the wall; it was 11:13 in the morning. I grabbed my purse and keys and headed out the door.

~ ~ ~ ~ ~

As I drove to the post office, I passed the school that I worked at. I hadn't been teaching for over six weeks now, and I missed it terribly. I made a mental note to call Principal Steve Clapton and tell him that I'd be back to work the following week. *Week? What day was it?* I had been mourning for so long, I hadn't recalled what day it was. Not that I really cared!

Once at the post office, I parked the car and dug in my purse looking for my cell phone that I wasn't sure I'd even put in my purse. It was. I pulled my phone out and was thankful that all cell phones had the date and time on them. I hit the side button on the phone, the screen lit up. It was Friday, April 10th. *April 10th,* I thought. *Had I really spent all that time in bed? A whole month?*

I knew I had a good reason to not get out of bed, but a month. I shook my head, clearing the thought. There was no reason to sit here and punish myself on what I'd already done. I didn't want to move on, especially without Tim, but what else could I do? He was gone, and so was my Mya. *Our Mya,* I corrected. That's what Tim had said to me after our last fight. It wasn't really a fight, more of a disagreement, maybe. He was angry with me, yes, but we weren't yelling and screaming at one another. I had simply said, *my Mya,* and he had slammed his fist on the table. Not that I hadn't seen that side of him before.

I opened the door and went inside.

Ten minutes later, I returned to my car and was now driving back towards home. As I came to a stop at the light, waiting to make the left onto my street, my body plunged forward as my car surged into the intersection. My head hit the steering wheel with abrupt force, before the seatbelt locked, jerking me back into the seat! I pressed down hard on the brake, trying to keep myself from becoming a target to the on-coming traffic.

When I came to a complete stop, I quickly jerked the shifter into park. I unhooked my seatbelt, rubbing my collarbone where it had dug into me. By the time I opened the door to get out, the woman from the other car came running towards me.

"I'm so sorry!" the woman exclaimed. "Are you okay? I should have been paying attention, instead of fumbling with the knob on my stereo. It was just for a split second that I took my eyes off the road," the woman sputtered, without taking a breath.

I leaned against my car, dizziness setting in. I could see the woman's mouth moving, but wasn't sure what she was saying. I grabbed for the car door, but wasn't able to grip anything before I went down. A second before I hit the ground, the woman with reddish-brown hair wrapped her arms around my mid-section and held me up.

"Here, let me help you sit back down," the woman offered.

Once back inside my car, I watched as the woman pulled out her cell phone and dialed a number. She was telling someone about the accident and where it was.

The ringing in my ears continued for a few more seconds, and then stopped. I raised my hand, gently touching my forehead.

"That's a nasty bump you have there," the woman testified. "My name is Michele, spelled with one "L" not two," the woman stated, before continuing. "I'll stay right by your side until the ambulance gets here. Don't need you falling out of the car, now do we?" Michele grinned.

I returned a smile, hoping this woman would stop talking. I hadn't even told the talkative woman… Wait, what was her name again? Oh, yeah, Michele. *Wait!* My mind yelled. Tim worked with a Michele, not that it could be the same woman. *What was it he had said she did? Was she an Attorney? No, that wasn't it. Adoptive parent? No, it was foster parent. She's a foster parent who was taking care of Samantha. Samantha,* I squeezed my eyes shut, wanting to block out what I'd read earlier.

"Are you okay, Miss?" Michele placed a hand on my shoulder.

"Yeah," I croaked. "Was just remembering something I didn't want to recall."

"I've had those days myself," Michele chuckled.

Sirens blared as they quickly approached the scene. The firetruck positioned itself in an angle in front of my vehicle, while the ambulance parked beside both of our cars. Within a few minutes, two police cars arrived at the scene.

I watched everything from the stretcher that the two men had placed me on. One of the police officers stood talking to Michele, while the other officer waved the cars around the accident. The two ambulance men lifted me up, placing me inside the rear of the truck. The short and slim nearly bald man climbed into the back and closed the door behind him.

Chapter 21

I rolled onto my side, trying to ease the discomfort in my back. The accident I was in earlier was showing its ugly face, as the pain worked itself up through my back to my neck. I didn't want to stay in the hospital, but the doctor had stated that it was best, due to the head trauma from the accident. Dr. Collins wanted to keep a close eye on me, just in case something happened.

I heard the door squeak open, but didn't move from my side to see who it was. It had taken me several excruciating minutes to get comfortable, why put myself through the pain again?

"Hey, Carla," Veronica said. "How are you doing?" She made her way around the bed and sat facing me.

I forced a smile, hoping my friend wouldn't notice how fake it was. "Hi," I whispered.

"I heard the news from Becky, whose husband works at the police station. As soon as work was over, I drove as quickly as I could to the hospital," Veronica stated.

I stared at her, not knowing what to say. Yesterday, I'd forced myself out of bed, to what?—end up back in the hospital. I wanted to go home. I wanted to curl up in my bed and never leave. I didn't care anymore!

What was I doing anyway? I should've stayed home and never gone to the office for Tim's things, then I wouldn't have gone to the post office and been in an accident, which put me back in the hospital. The last place I wanted to be! The place where Mya died.

I closed my eyes, trying to wipe my mind of the memories. Memories I didn't want to ever remember, again! *Like that was going to happen,* I thought.

I felt Veronica tuck a strand of hair behind my ear, and then smooth a finger over my cheek. "I'm so sorry, Carla. I wish I could make everything better," Veronica whispered.

A single tear escaped from under my closed eyelids. I just wanted to be alone, but didn't know how to tell my friend to leave. Was I wrong for wanting to be alone? To have no one around me because I was a total freaking mess! I wanted to tell Veronica to run away and never come back. That she'd be safer not to be around me.

I squeezed my eyes shut, trying to force the thoughts from my head, but they wouldn't leave. They wouldn't let me rest. I wanted to forget everything that had happened and everything I had learned in the past two months.

I could see a shadow move in front of me, and then it was gone, which meant, so was Veronica. Instead of confirming my friend had left, I remained lying in bed with my eyes closed.

$$\sim \; \sim \; \sim \; \sim \; \sim$$

The following afternoon, I called for a car to pick me up at the hospital and take me home. I knew I could've called Veronica, but I still wanted to be alone.

As the car pulled into my driveway, I saw my neighbor Deanna standing outside. I prayed silently that she wouldn't come over to talk to me. I climbed cautiously out of the car and coasted slowly up the walk to my front door. My back was still sore and moving too fast would have caused me more pain.

I unlocked the front door, closed it behind me, and rested my back against the door. I took in several calming breaths before walking into the kitchen. When my eyes caught sight of the table, I'd forgotten all about the things from Tim's office that were still scattered on the dinette. I turned away from the table and went straight to the cabinet beside the sink. I needed a painkiller.

I grabbed the bottle of Percocet from when I'd had the baby and deposited two in my palm, although the label read to only take one. I, on the other hand, just wanted to sleep and forget everything. I popped them in my mouth and washed them down with a glass of water. I won't lie, but part of me wanted to down the whole bottle.

After placing the cup in the sink, I turned and my eyes fell on a book that I hadn't remembered seeing before. It was sitting on the table with the rest of Tim's things from the office. *Had it been there the whole time? Had I just not paid attention to it before?*

Sure, that was possible. I had been engrossed in the file about Samantha, and then finding the DNA report the following day. It was definitely possible I hadn't noticed it before. I had been under a lot of emotional sadness with Tim's funeral and Mya's too. No one would expect me to bounce back in one day—surely, not even a week. Hell, I'd spent a month in bed, for crying out loud!

I slowly walked to the table and picked up the book. I glanced at the cover, but there was no title. I turned the book over, nothing on the back either. I flipped it back to the front and opened the cover. Tim's handwriting stared back at me. It looked like a journal.

I slammed the book closed! Did I have the right to read something that he had written in confidence? The right to invade his privacy? *Get real, Carla! Tim is dead!* The voice in my head shouted. *He's not going to get angry with you for reading it!*

"Of course, he can't," I laughed into the room. "It's not like he's a ghost or something. He won't haunt me."

I took in a deep breath, laughing at myself for thinking such foolishness. My body suddenly became heavy and sluggish. I set the book back down on the table and turned, walking out of the room and up the stairs to my bedroom.

$$\sim \sim \sim \sim \sim$$

I opened my eyes and glanced at the clock, it read 2:11. I searched the room to confirm if it was day or night. It was dark. I crept out of bed and used the bathroom before making my way downstairs. I flicked on the kitchen light, and then walked to the refrigerator for something to drink. Nothing appealed to me, and I decided to make some coffee.

Several long minutes later, the coffee maker sputtered to a finish. I had been leaning against the counter staring at the table with all of Tim's things. I turned, poured myself a cup, added some sugar and stirred. I hadn't realized I'd been in a trance until the *clanking* of the spoon against the ceramic mug brought me back.

I set the spoon on the counter and sat down in the chair. I took a sip from my cup, my eyes scanning over the items. Holding the mug in both hands, I took several more sips as I stared at the book. My mind was uncertain on what to do. *Should I open it and read his words?* Yes, of course, I should. I had the right to read his thoughts—his feelings. Right?

I shook my head. "Enough of this nonsense!" I mumbled. I set down the mug and with my left hand, touched the leather cover of the book. I smoothed my fingers against its soft texture, and then slid the book towards me. I opened the cover and read the words that flowed on the crème colored paper in front of me:

February 16th, 2015

I'm sitting beside my wife, who's still unconscious, watching as her eyelids flutter from time to time. It was just hours ago that I was sitting at my desk at the law firm, when the call came in that she was rushed to the hospital.

Veronica had called me, and was crying uncontrollably. At first, I had a hard time understanding a word she was saying. Once I was able to calm her down, she filled me in on what had happened at the school.

Veronica had told me that there was a gash on Carla's forehead, and she wasn't responding to her. Then the paramedics arrived and started working on Carla; they put her in an ambulance. That's when Veronica called me.

I heard Veronica sniffle through the phone placed at my ear, as I paced the room of my office.

I told Veronica that I was leaving work. Before I even had a chance to leave the office, the hospital called, telling me what I'd already known.

I'm thankful to have opened a law firm in Baker Park, maybe twenty minutes away from the hospital. Not that I minded getting up that extra hour earlier to catch the Metro train to downtown Chicago. At least not until all the trouble Carla was having with her pregnancies. I thought it was probably best to work closer to home. I went searching and found a reasonable lease on an office space near our house and opened my own law firm.

When I arrived at the hospital and entered the emergency room, the nurse behind the counter told me my wife was in surgery. The nurse added that the doctor on-call would need to speak to me once he was done in surgery. She handed me a few forms to fill out, and then went back to answering the phone.

I had glanced nervously around the waiting room; surprised not to see Veronica anywhere. I thought for sure she'd be here, waiting for me or for Carla to get out of surgery. I took a seat near the window; filled out the forms and handed them back to the nurse I'd talked to when I arrived.

Returning to the seat I was just sitting in, I tried to focus my attention on something, anything.

I was so nervous; I couldn't control my jittering leg. I hated hospitals; though I wasn't sure if it was because of all the times Carla and I had come to this hospital and left without a baby or was it that hospitals seemed so damn depressing as loved ones came to visit their sick and dying family member or friend? I didn't know, but I tried to stay positive and not think about her losing another baby.

It had crossed my mind a few times that maybe we weren't meant to be parents. I shook the thought from my head. No! I can't believe that for a minute!

Twenty minutes or so had passed, or maybe it had been hours, I wasn't sure. A man with short brown hair and a long white coat approached me. The doctor introduced himself and suggested that we talk in private. I followed Dr. Eugene Brooks through a set of doors, leading us into a small conference room.

As we walked, I noticed a clipboard clasped in the doctor's hand next to his side. I recalled signing some forms at the front desk to admit Carla into the hospital, but being a lawyer, I knew hospitals had to cover their ass if anything were to happen.

I turned my head when Dr. Brooks motioned to a set of chairs in the corner. I sat first, then Dr. Brooks.

At that moment, I could feel there was something wrong. My stomach began to feel queasy; I swallowed, forcing down the bile rising in my throat.

"My staff and I have sedated Carla and stopped the bleeding. When she was brought to the hospital, there was a gash on her forehead. We were told she'd most likely hit her head on something before falling to the floor, which in turn knocked her unconscious, but..." the doctor paused.

"But what?" I whispered, swallowing again.

"There was severe hemorrhaging in her abdomen. There's no easy way to say this. Carla has Placenta Increta.

It's where the placenta has difficulties separating from the uterine wall. In her case, the placenta attached too deep in the uterine wall and penetrated the uterine muscle. There would've been no other way except to deliver the baby through a C-section and do an emergency hysterectomy. I'm sorry," Eugene Brooks had said. "Your wife's life was at risk; we had to deliver the baby, or she would've died."

I could tell that Dr. Brooks was trying to sound sincere. Brooks had made eye contact and bowed his head after saying he was sorry.

"But Dr. Shaffer, our Gynecologist, told us the last time we saw him, she was fine, that the baby was fine! What changed? What happened to her? Did the baby survive?" I asked, almost pleading.

I had so many questions; I honestly didn't know where to start or what to ask first. They all just came fluttering out of me. I knew I needed to be the strong one. My wife would be devastated when she finds out the doctor had to perform a hysterectomy. My heart pounded hard in my chest. I wasn't sure how I would tell her.

"The baby is in NICU, Neonatal Intensive Care Unit. She's small, but

she's fighting for her life. As for what changed, I honestly don't know. A regular sonogram would have caught this, though there would've been nothing your doctor could've done, except to monitor the pregnancy. Sometimes these things just happen, and no one has or knows the answers to them," Dr. Brooks assured.

The doctor had said "she". That Carla and I had a daughter.

"A baby girl," I whispered, and then smiled, pushing the thought of the hysterectomy out of my mind.

"Before you go and sit with your wife, I need for you to sign these forms, which state that we performed an emergency hysterectomy on Carla Michaels."

I gripped the pen he handed me and signed my name on the dotted line, then followed the doctor to Carla's room.

* * *

I sit here replaying every word the doctor had said. I knew once she found out about the hysterectomy, especially if the baby doesn't survive, she'd plummet back into depression, again.

I don't have any other choice, but to tell her. Besides, it was better to hear it *from me and not the doctor. I had to keep in mind that the surgery had already been performed; there was no changing that.*

A hysterectomy? I wiped the tears from my cheek, and at the same time put a hand on my abdomen. Tim had written this when I was first put in the hospital. I hadn't thought about what he was going through. *Tim had to hold all that information in, afraid of what I'd do to myself,* I thought. But, he still should have told me the truth!

Was my friend Ashley right, had I been selfish and only thought about myself? I didn't stop to think how others would feel. How my husband felt about what I did or didn't do. I'd kept secrets from him as well, but nothing I thought would hurt him. If I'd told Tim about what our doctor had said, would it have saved Mya? Saved me from having a hysterectomy? Of course, I didn't know the answers to the questions, rolling around in my head. In all truth, I hadn't really known my husband.

Chapter 22

I stood from the chair and poured myself another cup of coffee. I hadn't realized that I'd finished the first cup, while reading the journal. I'd been engrossed in what my dead husband had written. Sitting back down, I opened the book to the next entry and started reading:

February 16th, 2015

I snapped back to the present when someone called out to me.

"Sir. Sir, would you like for me to bring you an extra blanket or something?" a nurse with short black hair asked.

I looked over at my wife, then back at the nurse. "Sure, that'd be nice. Thank you," I replied.

I stood up from the chair that I don't remember sitting in and stretched. I made my way back to the window and peered out. I wasn't sure when it had become dark outside.

I pushed the sleeve back on my arm and looked at my watch; the same watch Carla had given me for our eighth wedding anniversary. It was past ten in the evening. Have I really been sitting in that chair next to my wife for more than five hours?

I hadn't left the hospital since I'd arrived, nor did I leave the room to get something to eat, which come to think of it, I was hungry. The thoughts of food made my stomach growl.

I strolled back towards the bed, gently kissing her forehead, and walked out of the room towards the elevators.

* * *

February 17th, 2015

Carla finally opened her eyes this morning. We were talking, but mostly, I was inside my head still trying to figure out how to tell her the truth. A nurse startled me from my thoughts, when she walked into the room. I quickly stood and moved aside for her to check Carla's vitals.

My insides were still a jumbled mess from what the doctor had told me. My head pounded as I walked towards the window and looked out into the parking lot, replaying every word over and over again. I wasn't ready to tell her the truth, but could I keep it from her? She'd eventually find out, and it was in my best interest if I was the one who told her first.

An hour earlier, one of the nurses working on the floor took me to see our daughter for the first time. I can still picture her lying in the radiant neo-natal incubator—the nurse had called it, with two IV's going into her umbilical cord, a chest tube, endotracheal tube, and a feeding tube. Everything our daughter needed to stay alive.

I wasn't sure if I could handle losing another baby, even though I wanted a big family with lots of kids running around.

My strength and faith were barely holding on. After nine years of trying, it didn't seem possible that it would happen. Besides, Carla's health was more important than having a child, but I don't think she'll see it that way.

I wasn't sure if she knew, but whenever I was alone, I prayed. I'm not big in religious beliefs, but I still believe in God and Jesus. I prayed for her and for the baby she was carrying, I try to convince myself that if she lost, yet, another baby, that our marriage could handle the loss because after this baby, there's no more trying.

I've spent many hours thinking that we could adopt a baby or a child of any age. We never talked about adopting, mostly because I knew how bad Carla wanted to have her own baby. I'd have to find a way to convince her to do it.

I deal with cases all the time where kids are taken to foster homes due to their way of life. There were even some cases where a baby was brought in—the mother was either too young, or she just couldn't take care of a baby, and wanted a better life for her child.

~ ~ ~ ~ ~

I couldn't understand why my husband had never told me how he felt and what he thought. Maybe our marriage would've been different if he'd just talked to me about his feelings. I knew as well as anyone that I should've opened up to him too. We were both in the wrong, keeping things from one another.

I'd known about the Placenta being attached. My OB/GYN doctor had told me that much, but I didn't know the effect it would cause. I wasn't told that I could lose the baby the further along the pregnancy. I hadn't told Tim what the doctor had said; he had to find out about it through a different doctor, thinking to himself that I didn't know about it.

I didn't want to think about it, but if it weren't for Tim dying, would I have ever known about the hysterectomy? Sure, eventually my doctor would've told me. I would've found out! Anger was creeping up inside me, but now I blamed myself for what had happened. For my daughter dying.

Tim had kept this from me, when I should've been told the truth, and now…now I had to read about it in some stupid journal that he'd kept hidden away.

It was still dark outside when I decided to close the book. I didn't feel like reading anymore. I was emotionally drained and just wanted to crawl back into bed.

Chapter 23

It was after nine in the morning when I threw the blankets off and stepped out of bed. I padded to the bathroom and then made my way to the kitchen. I rinsed out the cup from earlier, refilled it with cold coffee, and placed it in the microwave. I wasn't awake enough to make a fresh pot.

I was glad that my body was feeling less achy than it had yesterday when I returned home from the hospital, or was it the two Percocet pills I'd taken? Were they still coating the pain? If that was the case, I'd just pop another pill later.

I turned and immediately saw the book I'd set aside hours ago. *Should I read more now, or wait until later? Now, wouldn't hurt,* I confirmed. I grabbed the cup from the microwave and sat at the table:

February 17th, 2015

I stare down the corridor after the nurse came and took Carla for some tests. I was so close to telling her about the hysterectomy the doctor had to perform. I let the last few words linger in my head, "had to perform". It wasn't like I'd given them permission; the surgery had **already** been done. I try hard to keep that in mind, but it continues to replay in my head, torturing me every minute. Eventually, I'll have to tell her the truth about what the doctor had told me yesterday.

* * *

When Dr. Brooks was in Carla's room and then was called for a code blue, I heard the room number and needed to know for sure if it was our baby's room.

I watched in horror through the window separating me from our daughter as they worked fast and efficiently to save her.

* * *

I think back to earlier, when I watched from a distance as Carla sat looking at our baby through the glass. Tears were falling down her face.

She hadn't known I was watching her from afar. I wanted to go up to her and comfort her, but I just couldn't. I *knew if I could fix her pain, I would, but I knew there was nothing I could do. I couldn't fix the baby. I wasn't God. I was just Carla's husband, standing in the distance, waiting for the right moment to tell her the truth. The truth that could bring her depression back. The same depression that had hospitalized her a year ago.*

* * *

My heart is warm inside as I stand watching my daughter. Every now and then, her fingers curl into a small fist and then unfold. Her tiny reddish feet were outstretched with one leg in a brace, along with a brace on her right arm. The nurse had told me earlier that she weighed one pound eight ounces and was thirteen inches long.

Right then and there, I prayed she'd survive to be able to go home with us soon. I didn't have to hold her to fall in love with her. Just one look was all it took for me to love her unconditionally.

* * *

Veronica just called me, asking if she could come and see Carla. I told her that she was getting some tests done and to come in a few hours to visit.

I stepped inside the elevator and rode down to the lobby and out the revolving doors of the main entrance.

The sun poked above the trees, warming my face as I looked up at the sky. I needed to get away for a while and collect my thoughts. I spent the night at the hospital and now, this morning, I needed time to myself. Too much was happening all at once, and I was afraid I'd burst into flames or something. Just for a while, I needed to have some time to myself.

* * *

When I arrived at the office, I poured myself a drink. Luckily, Pat Atkins, the one I share the lease with, is at court.

I sit down in a chair next to the window. I take a sip from my glass, the Black Velvet burning my throat as I swallow.

I need to talk to Carla before the doctor does, but I don't know how. How do I tell the one I love that we might never have a baby of our own? The whole thing torments me.

I move from the window to the chair at my desk. Turning on the lamp, I notice a light blinking on the office phone and press the button.

"Hey, it's me, Ashley. I tried calling your cell phone, but couldn't reach you. I'm glad I had your work number in my phone. Anyway, I just wanted you to know I will be driving to Illinois, but will probably stay the night in Indiana, depending how I feel. I'm thinking I'll be there sometime Thursday around noon, maybe sooner. I talked to Carla on the phone earlier and decided to surprise her by coming for a visit. So much has happened and I just need a break. Talk to you soon, bye."

I erase the message and sit back, taking another swig. Why would Ashley be coming out to see us? Maybe she knew about Carla and the baby? Maybe that's whom she'd called when I came into the room? If so, why wouldn't she have told me? I push the thought to the back of my mind and decide I'll ask her later when I go back to the hospital.

I take a long gulp, and then place the glass on the desk, empty. I don't drink often, only when I feel I need to take the edge off. Something, I'm grateful, I didn't get from my father.

I can feel a buzz, coursing through my veins and fogging up my head. I don't want to take the chance driving so I fumble through a few files, trying to clear my mind.

I spend most of the day at the office and know I should get back to the hospital before it gets too late. It's not that I need to, but I want to be with my wife. She's already tried calling me on my cell, but I can't make myself answer it so I let it go to voicemail.

Ever since we met in college, we've never been apart from each other. Besides going to work, we spend all our time together. I know I'm not going home to an empty house and sleep in our bed without her.

* * *

February 18th, 2015

I open the door to my office and close it behind me. I take a seat at my desk, pick up a file, and start reading about a new case that was given to me. The last name on the file reads "Berkley" and that the child is seven-years old and lives with both parents.

The report from the police says, "possible child abuse".

My heart sinks at the thought of someone abusing his or her child. I look at the photos inside the file, and then read more of the report. The feeling of disgust runs through me.

"The child was taken from the home and rushed to the hospital. Ms. Samantha Marie Berkley will be placed in the care of Michele Channels, a court-approved foster parent. The child will remain with her foster parent until further notice." Which to me meant, until she is adopted or another family member comes and takes her in. I close the file and push away from the desk.

* * *

I needed a little nap before I headed back to the hospital. I make my way to the sofa along the far wall in my office and lie down.

I didn't sleep more than a couple of hours last night. I spent most of my time watching Carla sleep or walking down to NICU to look at Mya through the glass window.

I wanted so much to hold her in my arms, to protect her from harm, but *there was nothing I could do. I'll have to wait until she gets stronger and doesn't need all those machines attached to her body. In the back of my mind, I knew that could be months down the road, **if** she survived.*

I folded my right arm behind my head and looked up at the ceiling. I just needed a couple more hours of sleep, and then I'd feel better and could get some work done.

The phone rang, startling me, and I fell off the couch. I quickly scrambled to my feet, grabbed the chair in front of me, and reached for the phone on my desk.

I answered, sounding out of breath as my heart pounded in my chest. It was Michele Channels, the foster parent I work with. She was calling to ask me about the "Berkley case". She wanted to know if I'd read the reports and to tell me that I needed to go visit this little girl in the hospital. The same hospital Carla was in.

Michele told me that the case would be going in front of a judge in a couple of weeks. Michele needed me to make sure they didn't get custody of their daughter again. I also needed to get ahold of Pat Atkins and see what we could dig up on her parents. Michele said that the police should have photos of the little girl and asked me to see if I could get some copies for our records.

Before getting off the phone, for the first time since Carla had been taken to the hospital, no one had asked how I was doing. I didn't even know how I was doing. With my main concern for my wife and Mya, I didn't have time to think about myself.

*So, I told Michele that I was doing fine and started to tell her about Carla, but she interrupted me and said that she wasn't asking about her; she said that my wife was being taken care of, but who was taking care of me? She went on to say, **"I know what you have done for her, the sacrifices you have made, but you need taken care of too. It's not a one-sided marriage."***

Michele said she wasn't trying to butt in; she was just trying to be a friend. Besides, she knew me better than anyone.

"Take some time for yourself,"** Michele said. **"This baby thing from the start has had you under so much stress. When will you ever sit down and talk to Carla about everything?"

I replied that it wasn't as easy as she thinks, and that I love Carla and wanted her to be happy. Then Michele said, **"Shouldn't you be happy too? Shouldn't she know about your past and what you've done?"**

I quickly said that I was happy in a way. Although I was frowning, I started to pace the room. I wasn't good at sharing my feelings, especially with Michele who had been there in the past. I made one mistake, maybe two, that was telling Michele what I was feeling, and now it felt like she was throwing it back in my face.

Michele added, **"Just take care of yourself and be honest with Carla."**

I told her I had been honest with my wife, as I continued to pace the room. She started going on about the baby possibly dying and the hysterectomy that Carla was given. She told me I needed to talk to my wife before she ended up back where she was a year ago.

I stopped pacing and rubbed my forehead with my free hand. Not that it relieved the stress. I honestly didn't feel like having this conversation, at least not today. Not with Michele. "I said I'd talk to her!" I snapped.

I knew that I was starting to lose it. The stress of everything that I was holding inside was on the verge of bubbling out.

Before getting off the phone, she told me to keep in mind how many children are out there that need homes. Parents who would love them and wouldn't hurt or desert them.

I hung up the phone and glanced down at the Berkley file on my desk, and then I called Pat Atkins.

* * *

Forty-five minutes later, I parked the car and climbed out, making my way towards the hospital doors. I saw Pat standing in the smoking section, a cigarette between his fingers.

I mentioned that I thought he had quit smoking. Pat pleaded that he had quit, but liked to hold an unlit cigarette between his fingers.

I watched as he stuck the unlit cigarette back in the pack, and slid it into his pants pocket.

We both walked through the doors of the hospital and towards the receptionist desk. I knew after meeting with the Berkley girl, I should go see how Carla was doing. Although I'd just left her side a couple of hours ago, I still felt guilty for working on a new case. My wife and daughter needed me, but I needed to keep my mind focused on other things. It was my way of coping with stress and sadness. A life that I'd come accustomed to.

I leaned against the counter, while Pat asked the older woman sitting behind the desk for the room number. Once Pat had the number, we walked casually towards the elevator and rode to the fifth floor.

** * **

I don't really know how to explain the feelings I'm having after seeing and talking to Samantha Berkley. The bruises on her face take me back to when I was a child. My father was not one to hold back when he felt like punching something. I had always seemed to be there when he needed to let off some steam, so to speak.

I touch my left forearm where it had once been snapped apart. The bone protruded through the skin. I, of course, had told the teachers I had fallen off my bike, but really my father had actually taken a bat to me that day. The sad part is, I'll never forget each and every time my father abused me.

Chapter
24

I quickly stood and ran to the sink. I turned on the water waiting to vomit, but had only dry heaves. I wasn't sure why I felt sick after reading what Tim had written. Maybe it was because I never knew that my husband was abused, and that the thought of it made my stomach do summersaults.

He'd never told me. *But why?* Why did he feel the need to hold all of this in and not confide in me? Instead, I had to read about it in his journal. Part of me felt angry with him for doing this. For not trusting me with his life!

Wiping my hands with the dishtowel, I straightened and leaned against the counter. I wasn't sure if I could read anymore, but mostly, I hated reading Tim's final words, when he could have just talked to me. *Why hadn't he confided in me? Had I really been so consumed with myself that he couldn't talk to me? In the whole time we'd been married, he couldn't find the right time, the right words to tell me?* It disgusted me to find out this way. Tim had confided in this Michele Channels woman, but not me. His own wife!

My thoughts went back to the accident a couple of days ago. It was the first time I'd met this Michele Channels, but my sight and thoughts were fuzzy. I wasn't sure if it was the same *Michele* that Tim knew. I didn't really get a good look at her, didn't understand what she was saying. The only thing I really remembered was that she sure did like to talk.

I jumped when I heard a knock on the front door. I glanced down at my body to make sure I was presentable. I was still wearing the robe I'd put on a couple of hours ago. I grabbed the straps on each side and pulled them tight.

The knock came again, before I had a chance to get to the front door. When I opened the door, a woman with reddish-brown hair stood on the porch. She looked vaguely familiar to me, but I couldn't quite put my finger on who she was.

The woman tilted her head to one side, as if realizing that we've met before, too. "Is there a Carla Michaels that lives here?" the woman asked.

I nodded, "Yes, I'm Carla Michaels. What can I help you with?"

"I think we met the other day. I'm the one who accidentally rear-ended you," the woman smiled slightly, holding out her hand.

"Oh," I replied, unsure if I should shake her hand.

"I don't know if you remember me from the other day, but my name is Michele Channels. I worked with your husband, Tim," she stated. "If you don't mind, I'd like to have a word with you?"

"Um, sure. Please, come in." I moved to the side, allowing Michele to enter into the foyer. "Sorry about the mess," I blurted out. I wasn't sure why I felt the need to offer that information. The house wasn't a disaster or anything, though it could use a bit of a dusting, maybe a vacuum.

Michele stood in front of me not saying a word. This was different from the other day when she hit my car. She was much more talkative and wouldn't shut up, and now she was as quiet as a mouse on a cold winter's day.

"What did you need to talk about?" I asked.

"Is there somewhere we can sit down?" Michele responded.

"Sure." I led Michele into the kitchen. When I spotted the table covered with Tim's things, my face became hot. "Sorry, I'll just move some things aside." I quickly grabbed the book and made sure the file was hidden away inside the box.

"I'll…I'll… st…start a pot of coffee," I stuttered. "Would you like a cup? Guess I should've asked you that first," I smirked, feeling embarrassed.

"If it's no problem, that'll be great, thanks," Michele smiled as she looked around the room, before taking a seat at the table.

I turned and walked to the sink. I dumped out the old coffee, filled the pot with fresh water, and scooped in new coffee grounds. "It'll be a few minutes before it's finished, is there anything else I can get you while we wait?"

"No, I'm fine; thank you for asking."

I sat down across from Michele. "So, what is it you'd like to talk to me about?" I shifted in my chair, while tucking some hair behind my ear, hoping that it wasn't a mess.

"Well, we've never formally met when Tim and I worked together. I just thought it'd be nice to finally meet you. I'm really sorry about the other day. How are you feeling?"

Now, I recalled that woman from the accident. *She must have found her tongue,* I thought. "I'm feeling a little better. Still sore in some places, but I'll manage."

"Again, I'm so sorry for hitting your car. I didn't see it in the driveway. I hope I didn't burden you and leave you without transportation. That would be a shame, ya' know, not having a way to get around," Michele nodded and continued talking. "Here I go rambling on and on again. I'm so sorry I can't seem to shut my mouth sometimes, ya' know. It's like, I have all these things I want to say, and when I finally get to say them, I just can't seem to shut my big fat mouth. There I go again, doing that rambling thing again." Michele stopped talking immediately, and opened her large over-sized purse, which looked more like a tote bag, and pulled out a thick envelope. "My main purpose was to come here and give you this. For some reason someone had it mailed to my house, instead of to yours," Michele stated, then handed me the parcel. "I'm not sure what's in it, but again, I'm assuming it's extremely important since **Important** is written in bold letters across the front. I noticed it said c/o Carla Michaels, under my name and figured I'd just bring it to you."

I grabbed the envelope and placed it in my lap, then looked back up at Michele. "Oh, well, thank you for bringing it over to me," I swallowed.

The coffee came to a sputtering stop; I was feeling uncomfortable and quickly stood, setting the envelope down on the table, and went to the counter. I poured two cups, set them on the table and went back for the sugar and cream. My mind kept replaying what Tim had written that Michele had said to him. From what I got from his words, it sounded like Michele didn't like me. Not that I knew her. Hell, we hadn't officially met until today.

I sat back down at the table, silence filling the air as we both stirred our coffee. I took a sip, set the cup back on the table, but still holding onto it at the same time. Before I could speak, Michele spoke first.

"I'm not sure why I'm going to tell you this, but I've had many conversations about you with Tim. I guess, what I'm trying to say is that I shouldn't have taken his word about you, or even judged you without ever meeting you," the corner of Michele's lips curled up.

I was speechless. It was almost like this woman could read my mind. I was just thinking the same thing.

"I know I've done all the talking since I arrived here, but like I said, feel free to tell me to shut my mouth as I can talk your ear off if you let me."

"If you don't mind, I'd like to ask you a few questions?" I chirped.

"Well, sure, ask away."

"Well, first," I started to say. "How well did you know my husband, Tim?" I wasn't sure if I was ready for whatever answer Michele was going to give me in return, but I figured, why not? She was here in my home, and plus I'd just read the journal about Michele, so why couldn't I ask whatever I wanted to? I did have the right to know what my husband was thinking, what he'd gone through.

Michele's face fell flat. "Oh, well, I wasn't expecting that. I've known Tim since he was eight years-old."

"Eight?"

"Yeah, that's when he was brought to me by the courts. He was taken away from his father."

"Why? What did his father do to him?" I knew what Tim had written down, but I wanted to hear what Michele had to say, praying I could hold my own and not get sick again.

"Tim's father used to abuse him. Mentally and physically."

"What do you mean *mentally*? What did he say to him?" I asked, before taking a sip of my coffee.

Michele did the same before answering the question. "His father used to tell him that he wasn't worth his time and that nobody would want him. That he was a worthless kid who didn't deserve to be loved by anyone, and that he was a mistake. His father also told him that he wished he were never born. That he let his dick do the talking, when he should've kept his penis in his pants where it belonged, instead of screwing Tim's mother."

I wasn't sure what to say. The words still fresh in my mind. *Tim's own father didn't want him! Didn't love him!*

"I take it, you didn't know any of this," Michele replied, squeezing my hand.

I shook my head.

"Well, just so you know, it was a good thing that Tim was taken out of that house when he did. He grew up to be a great man. A man who would love anyone, with or without flaws."

My head jolted up from the comment, looking at Michele. "What does that mean?" I snapped. "What did he tell you about me that would make you say something like that?"

"I'm not sure what you're getting at?" Michele questioned, sounding offended. "Yes, Tim and I talked, but he didn't tell me anything he didn't want me to know. Besides, he needed to talk to someone about what happened a year ago," Michele hissed.

I immediately jumped to my feet. "I think it's time for you to go!" I pointed to the front door.

I watched as Michele's mouth dropped open, and then grabbed her handbag from the side of the chair and stood. "I'm..."

I pursed my lips. I didn't need to say any words to tell Michele that she should leave now, before I exploded!

"Good day, then," Michele mumbled as she walked out the door.

Chapter 25

I slumped down into the chair in the kitchen, my body convulsing as I started to cry. Tim had told Michele about what I'd done a year ago. Something that was supposed to be kept a secret! Even the school hadn't known about it; otherwise I would've lost my teaching job. Was that why I had waited until school was out? So, they wouldn't have known what I'd done? However, they would've if I'd achieved my goal. *Goal*, like it was something I'd wanted my whole life.

"What a stupid thought," I mumbled.

I wiped the tears from my face and reached for the book, noticing the parcel that Michele had given me. Changing my mind, I tore the large envelope open and reached inside. I pulled out several medium sized books with a letter.

```
     To whom it my concern:

     I'm the executive in-charge
  of Tim Michaels's estate, and
```

was instructed to send out this and many other envelopes every few days, if, and when, death has occurred. If you should have any questions regarding what is in this envelope, please read the enclosed letter that Tim Michaels has written.

Sincerely, my condolences,
Attorney Robert Beckon.

I set the letter aside and opened the first book. Just like the Attorney had written, there was a folded letter inside. I took in a deep breath and opened the letter:

My Dearest Carla,

If you are reading this, then something has happened to me. I left this because I wanted you to know the real me.

When I was eight years old, the parents you know, adopted me. They saved me from a lifelong abuse that my real father was inflicting on me. I was mentally and physically abused by him; there were some instances that he even sexually abused me.

It is taking everything that I have to write this letter to you and tell you of my past that I have kept a secret from you. It wasn't that I didn't love you enough. It was that I didn't want to lose you!

A year ago, you were in a different place, why? I'm still unsure. I showed you all the love that I have inside of me and couldn't possibly give you more, as it was all I had to give you. You were my life, my soul mate that I wanted to live my whole life with.

I decided to leave you some journals of mine, so you can get to know the Tim Michaels you were meant to know and love. I just hope after you've read them, you still feel the same as you did ten years ago.

Also, my darling, Carla, you will always be a part of me wherever I am. I love you more than you love yourself, but I hope after reading these, you will find it in yourself to love again, and to be happy for once in your life.

I'll love you forever and always,

Tim

A tear dropped from my chin onto the paper. My heart was heavy with sadness, and I wished I didn't have to sit here and read a letter from a man I whole-heartedly loved. No matter what I'd felt before, it wasn't what I was feeling now, or ever for that matter. I did love Tim. I had always loved Tim. Now, as time stood still, I had to keep myself together and find *my* real Tim.

Thursday, 1/5/84

My new mom and dad said I could get whatever I wanted; I chose a journal to keep all of my thoughts in. I got the idea from the therapist I have to go see every week. The one who listens to whatever I feel like sharing when I go.

I was glad when I first walked into the room that it was a woman and not a man therapist. I don't feel very comfortable around men, well except for my new dad. He's really nice and before he touches me, he lets me know what he's going to do so I don't panic. Mostly, he just likes to hug me. He does that a lot since I came to live with them.

Their house is huge, with six bedrooms and seven bathrooms. I have actually gotten lost in the house. Maybe a few days had gone by before I didn't anymore. They let me choose my room and asked me what color I wanted it to be.

They hired some painters and colored the walls a blue color.

They bought me all kinds of toys, though I didn't have the heart to tell them they didn't have to buy me things. I didn't want them to get mad at me.

I start at a new school on Monday. I'm a little nervous, but they said everything would be fine, so I'll have to write about my first day of school.

Well, I have to go, my new mom is calling me for dinner.

*** * ***

Monday, 1/9/84

School was awesome!! I made a new friend, named Sean, which I'm thrilled about, since I didn't have any at my last school. Mostly, because I was afraid to bring them to my house. I didn't want my real dad to hurt them like he did me.

My teacher is very nice and she told me that I'm a bright student. Not like 'bright', I'm colorful, bright. I know she meant that I am very smart. They had me take this test today. I think I was the only one who had to take it because I didn't see anyone else in the room with me, except another teacher. After, I finished the test the woman in the room took me back to where the other kids were.

At lunch is when I met my new friend. His name is Sean Bailey, and he was nice to me and let me sit with him at lunchtime. Then we played ball at recess with some other kids.

I'll close for now. My mom says it's time for bed.

* * *

Friday, 1/13/84

Sean was freaking out today because it's Friday the 13th, but I don't see how that's a scary day. I mean, it's Friday. Every week we have a Friday; does that mean it's scary every Friday? Then he tells me it's because it's the 13th, and that bad things happen to people on that particular day, especially when the 13th is on a Friday. He said I should come over to his house and we can watch the movie together, so I can see what he's talking about.

Mom said we could go over after dinnertime, so I need to have a bag packed for a sleepover. This will be my first sleepover ever! I'm going to leave my journal home, though. I don't want anyone to read what I write. Mom's calling, gotta go.

* * *

Saturday, 1/14/84

Oh, my gosh! I had so much fun at Sean's place. His mom ordered pizzas, and we stayed up until two in the morning, watching Friday the 13th movies. Those movies freaked me out! I didn't get much sleep after we watched all four movies in a row. I kept thinking Jason was going to come after me, so I pretended to be asleep, so the other boys wouldn't make fun of me.

When my mom asked what we did, I told her we watched those movies, she didn't seem too happy about that, but she did tell me there was nothing to be scared about because it was all fake. She said that those people are actors, and that the blood wasn't real. I don't know if I could be an actor and do those kinds of things. Besides, I already know what I want to be when I get older, a Lawyer.

I noticed that Tim had changed how he dated each section in his journal. Something that he'd probably changed later in life, I presumed.

I read the journal until mid-day. I didn't stop to eat or get anything to drink. I was fascinated by what Tim wrote when he was only eight. I smiled at times when I was amazed at his imagination. His writing intrigued me and kept me wanting to read more of his life. He hadn't told me any of this. It was like reading about someone I never met before.

By the time I read the first book, it was past seven in the evening. I didn't want to stop and decided to take them upstairs and finish them in bed.

Tuesday, 1/17/84

Tonight is therapist night. I think I'll bring my journal with me so I can read some things to my doctor. She had said I could and wants to know what I have been feeling and thinking lately.

I don't know if I'll share the parts of me that are still scared that my real dad will come and take me away from my new family. I don't want him to. I really like it here and want to stay.

At dinnertime, my new mom and dad like to share their day with me. They say I should be open and share what I've done at school and any thoughts I may have that are concerning to me. Like if something were bothering me. I don't want them to be mad at me. I don't want to be punished, again. I don't want them to send me back to my real dad!

Gotta go for now, we're off to see my therapist.

When I turned the page the date skipped to mid-February. For a whole month, he'd written nothing, and then started again. I had to continue to find out. To me, it felt like a mystery novel, except it was about my husband.

Sunday, 2/19/84

I know I haven't written in my journal in a while. My therapist says that I should keep writing no matter what I'm feeling inside or how busy I am.

Besides school, I've been busy trying out for baseball. I'm not that good. I'm mostly doing it because Sean wants me to, so we can spend more time together. He says that playing a sport will "toughen me up", but I don't want to be tough, I just want to be normal, feel normal.

What is feeling and being normal really like, anyways? To feel normal, I would have to be excited and happy all the time, wouldn't I? Some days, I don't feel like doing anything. My mom says I may be feeling a little depressed. I don't know what depressed means. I guess, sort of, like I am sad.

I'm not sure why I'd be sad. I have a great home and two parents that are nice to me and give me things, and I guess they love me.

The therapist said that I may be having some kind of withdrawal from my abusive father. Being treated one way and then moving and actually being loved in another way. My mind doesn't know what's right or wrong.

*I know I don't want to move back with my real father. I don't want to be hit or locked in the closet for hours and days at a time. And, I definitely don't want to be touched on certain parts of my body that the doctor said is **wrong**!*

What actually is being normal? I go to school just like I used to do, though I don't have to hide any bruises or broken bones. I don't think I'm being anything but normal.

There are things that I am afraid of, and things I don't understand, but my mom says that I am too young to understand what is happening in my mind. That once I feel safe, I will be safe; whatever that means.

* * *

Tuesday, 2/21/84

I have to stay home from school today because I'm running a fever and have a sore throat. My mom says she doesn't want me to spread my germs around to the other students.

I don't feel like writing today because I feel tired, but I have to do what my therapist says so I can get better. I'll write more later.

* * *

Wednesday, 2/22/84

I'm still in bed, sicker than I was yesterday. My mom says she's going to take me to the doctor later and find out what's wrong with me.

Well, it turns out I have Strep throat. The doctor gave me some antibiotics to help me get better and said I should stay home from school because I am very contagious.

Sean called a little while ago and said he was going to come over and drop off the assignments that the teachers gave him for me.

My mom told him that he wouldn't be able to visit with me. She doesn't want him to get sick.

When I heard Sean come to the door, I got out of bed and we waved to each other from my bedroom window. I miss hanging out with him. I hope I get better soon.

I was snuggled under the blankets when I finished the second journal and started on the third one. I read until my eyes became heavy.

Chapter 26

The following morning, I crept out of bed and made my way downstairs. All was silent, except for the *crackling* and *moaning* of the house waking up.

The sun beamed through the curtains in the kitchen as I poured a cold cup of coffee and reheated it in the microwave. I stretched and leaned against the counter, waiting for it to finish.

Since Michele had stopped over yesterday, I hadn't showered or changed my clothes. I just sat reading through Tim's journals. Remembering the letter from the Attorney, it stated that there would be more journals of Tim's, arriving every few days. *How many had he written?* I thought. Well, if he continued since the age of eight, and he was thirty-five when he died, there could be hundreds of journals.

The microwave beeped, I grabbed my cup and sat down at the table. Yesterday, I was reading one of his journals from the past couple of months and decided to finish reading what was left.

I stood and pulled the box towards me. I peered inside, grabbed the book, and sat back down. I thumbed through the pages until I found where I'd left off.

February 20ᵗʰ, 2015

Carla's home from the hospital now, and her friend, Ashley Teodora, from Ohio, came to visit her. I've been busy with a new case, which I'm glad of since Mya is still in the hospital, for who knows how long.

I go to the hospital several times a day when Carla doesn't know I'm there. I go to see Mya, and to hold her in my arms. I hope she'll survive because I love her more than anything, but if she doesn't, then I hope I can survive without her.

Carla seems distant lately, now that she's home. I hope she doesn't push me away, again. Yesterday, I overheard her tell Ashley that she wasn't happy. I came home for lunch to surprise her, and that's when I heard her say those hurtful words, again. I made my way into the kitchen so she'd see that I was home and that I'd heard what she'd said.

I asked Ashley to give us a minute to talk and waited for her to leave the room. Once she left, I almost crumbled to the floor. I wanted to, but I knew I had to be the strong one. I was the one who had to hold it together. I used everything inside me to move forward and sit across from my wife.

I wish I could have been more open with her, but with her past, I was afraid to show that side of me. I knew at that moment if Mya died, so would Carla. There would be no way she'd survive another death. Carla—I knew wasn't strong enough.

After we talked and I got her to agree on getting some help, some counseling, we left and went to the hospital to see Mya.

It wasn't until I was alone that I crumbled. I cried like a baby in my car, my head in my hands. That's when I knew that she needed to know the real me and what I had to endure.

*** * ***

February 23rd, 2015

I've been working on this new case about a little girl named Samantha. She was being abused by both her parents and was finally taken out of the home, and her parents were arrested. My partner, Pat Atkins, and I have been digging up whatever we could on the parents, so they wouldn't get custody of their daughter again.

When I first saw a picture of Martha, she looked vaguely familiar to me, like I'd seen her somewhere before. I couldn't quite put my finger on it and moved on to some searches.

Once I started doing some research on Martha Berkley, Samantha's mother, I stumbled across two forms that were filed. One, Martha's name was listed in an obituary when her mother and father were killed in a car accident when she was fourteen, but it was her mother's name that had me puzzled, <u>Lisa Blackstine</u>. Second, Martha had married John Berkley. She was once known as <u>Kathy Sonnets</u> almost eight years ago.

Tim had underlined the two names as if they meant something to him, but I couldn't remember anything written in the file with those names, nor did he say whom the people were. I'd read over the paragraph twice, and it still left me confused and yet, eager to find out the truth.

I'd sent out the DNA test; the same test that had Samantha and Martha's results on it. *Why hadn't Tim sent in his DNA at the same time?* I thought. None of this was making sense to me, but I was going to make it my priority. I would finish what Tim started.

When I turned the page to continue reading, I found it blank. I flipped through several more pages, there was nothing! I had come to the end of Tim's recent diary. Other than the journals from his youth, I wouldn't be able to read his innermost thoughts.

A thought came to me; I tipped the box towards me and pulled out Samantha's case file. I quickly shuffled past the photos of Samantha and scanned over what Tim had written down. I stopped when the handwriting changed. The date written was March 13th 2015.

"The day Tim had died," I whispered. Tim hadn't written anything about the DNA test, or that Martha Berkley could be related to him—in some way. I scanned over the rest of the file, which it had occurred to me was probably Pat Atkins handwriting, since they had worked on the case together.

My finger stopped when I found what I was looking for. I stood and hurried over to a drawer in the kitchen, pulling out a notepad and pencil. Sitting back down, I wrote down all of Martha's information: what prison she was at, birthdate, and any known relatives; anything I could find on this woman. When I finished, I made my way upstairs to wash up.

$$\sim \sim \sim \sim \sim$$

As I came bouncing down the stairs, I knew there was something different inside me. Something I hadn't felt in a very long time, confidence, and maybe even a little cheerfulness. I wanted to think the word *happy*, but I didn't want to confuse the two. I knew that happiness was something you had to find inside yourself; something I had trouble doing. If I were to be *happy,* I wouldn't be allowed to have negative thoughts about myself. I would have to for once—love myself.

I grabbed a warmer jacket from the hall closet. The temperatures had been bouncing from the forties to the seventies this past week. There were even days the sun hadn't shown its face. It was better to wear something warm, then to not and be cold.

Purse in hand, I opened the front door and realized I didn't have a car. I had been sent straight to the hospital, without knowing where my car was. I also hadn't left the house since I came home from the hospital.

I closed the door and walked back to the kitchen, where I found Tim's keys hanging on a hook. I wrapped my slim fingers around them, closed my eyes, and blew out a breath.

I hadn't been in his car since… *No, I can't think about that now!* I'd deal with the emotions later. Right now, I was on a quest. I wanted and needed to find the answers that Tim wasn't able to accomplish. It would be my gift to him.

I opened the car door; the smell of my husband embraced me. It took everything inside me not to break down and cry. After several deep breaths, I climbed inside and started the engine, and typed the address in the navigator. According to the map, I had a two-and-a-half-hour drive ahead of me. I backed out of the driveway and drove towards I-80 west.

~ ~ ~ ~ ~

A little over two hours later, I took Exit 135 towards the Dakar and Bloomingbird area. A few left and right turns later, I was pulling into the parking lot of Dakar Correctional Center for Women.

I put the car in park and sat back in my seat. I knew I had to go through with this. I had driven one hundred and thirty-one miles; there was no changing my mind, no going back. I thought of Tim and the unanswered questions that remained unsolved.

"I can do this," I soliloquized. "I'm strong. I'm confident." I thought saying the words aloud would make them more true—more alive.

I gathered the paperwork I'd brought and opened the car door. Once inside the main entrance of the prison, my heart raced, causing sweat to form along my hairline and run down my neck. The place was setup like the security line at an airport, but with more police officers. I had to have my purse searched and lay everything I'd brought with me on a conveyor belt.

I blew out a breath, walked up to the guard. The officer patted me down and then I had to go through a metal detector. *I guess they want to make sure I'm not bringing something into the prison that could be used as a weapon or even drugs for the in-mate I was here to see,* I thought.

I'd never been to a prison before so I wasn't sure if this was standard procedure. I gathered my belongings and walked up to one of three windows along the wall.

"Who are you here to see?" asked the middle-aged woman behind the glass.

"Oh, um, Martha Berkley," I responded.

"I'll need two forms of identification, such as a driver's license, passport, a state ID card, government ID card, military ID/driver's license, which must contain your date of birth," the woman said, as if it were a recording.

I hadn't known what to bring and started searching my purse. I pulled out my wallet and handed the woman my driver's license and auto insurance card."

"Auto insurance card isn't a proof of ID, ma'am."

"Oh," I spat and thumbed through my wallet for something else. I found my teacher's ID, took a quick glance, and handed it to the woman.

"Thank you, Miss Michaels," the woman growled.

I looked down at my hands, automatically thinking how rude the woman was being towards me. *Maybe she'd woken up on the wrong side of the bed,* I noted. I listened as the woman tapped away at the keys, waiting for her to finish.

As I waited, I ease-dropped on a conversation behind me. Two women, probably mothers visiting their daughters, were bickering about the visiting hours, which I hadn't even thought about when I climbed into the car and drove here. I hadn't really thought about anything, except finding answers. I got lucky, having two ID's on me. I wouldn't have been too happy driving all the way home, and then having to drive all the way back down here. Not that I had anything else to do.

The woman slid my cards back under the glass. "You'll have to place your purse in a locker and make sure that all paper clips and staples are removed from the papers in your hand. Once you're done with that, the guard at the end of the hall will open the door to the visiting room," the woman preached.

I grabbed my cards and stepped away from the window. I turned and saw a row of lockers along the wall. After placing my handbag inside locker twenty-one, I went through the papers in my hand, removing all staples and paperclips. I closed the locker door and turned the key, placing it in the front pocket of my jeans. Before approaching the officer, I dumped the small handful of staples into the trashcan.

The officer asked for my key and stated that I would get it back after my visit. He opened the door, and I walked slowly inside the visitor's room, scanning the scenery. I didn't know what Martha looked like; there were no photos inside the case file of her. I decided to take a seat at an abandoned table and wait for her. *"What if she's already in here, waiting for me?"* I thought to myself, and then started scoping out the room.

I didn't notice anyone sitting alone, which made me feel more out of place. A door near the back wall opened, and a woman wearing an orange jumper came trotting in like she owned the place. The woman looked around and then met my eyes.

I raised my hand and waved "hello", smiling at the same time. Once I realized what I was doing, I dropped my hand and bowed my head as if I was being scorned. I probably looked like a stupid fool, waving like that. When I looked back up, Martha was standing by the table, glaring down at me.

"Who the hell are you?" Martha howled.

I swallowed, my hands trembling. I quickly placed them on my lap, out of sight from Martha. I didn't want her to see how frightened, how scared, I was to be here next to her. I cleared my throat, "My name is Carla Michaels. My husband Tim was an attorney in your daughter's case. Samantha Berkley is your daughter?" I finished in a question.

"What do you care if she is or isn't?" Martha barked back at me.

"Please sit. I'd like to talk to you about something."

Martha looked as if she was contemplating the thought, and after a couple seconds, she sat down across from me. "What do you want?" Martha questioned.

"Well," I paused, clearing my throat, "I was reading over your file and came across something that bothered me." I swallowed. "Tim did a DNA test on you and Samantha. I believe it shows that you are her mother, but…but I don't think he did the test to find that out. I believe that it's possible you two may be related somehow."

"What would make you think this?" Martha replied.

I shuffled through the papers on the table, "He found this while doing a search on you."

I watched as Martha read over the paper. "What does this prove? I have no idea who this woman is. She definitely ain't my mother. I've never heard of her in my life," Martha stated.

"Okay, maybe he was wrong," I tapped my finger on the table, "but there's definitely something between you two, and I'm going to find out. I'm going to do what my dead husband was trying to uncover himself."

"What do you mean *dead* husband?"

"Tim was shot by your husband during the court procedures. Your husband, John, killed him, but was shot and killed in the process by one of the officers in the courtroom."

"Oh, well, I guess he shouldn't have been there then. Sometimes John can lose his temper, and there's no way to stop him when he's angry."

For a second, I thought I could hear sincerity in Martha's voice, but that second ran short.

"I suppose Tim, that's your husband's name, right?"

I nodded.

"Tim was just a lucky son of a bitch!"

"Lucky!" I swallowed, trying hard to hold back; I failed terribly. "Your husband shot him and you say he's *lucky*!" My voice rose. "That has to be the meanest thing anyone has ever said! You know what?" I stood, my temper rising. "You deserve to be here. I hope that you rot in hell for what you did to that little girl!" I grabbed the papers from the table, turned on my heels, and stomped out of the room. I wanted nothing more to do with that…that woman!

I grabbed my things from the locker and fled the building. It wasn't until I was in the comfort of Tim's car that I released the tears I fought so hard to hold inside. For a brief moment, I understood some of what Tim had gone through. The things he held inside, never letting them out. I wasn't sure how he did it all those years. I, on the other hand, would've gone out of my mind.

I wiped the tears from my face and started the car. My mind, for some reason, remembered reading that Martha Berkley had gotten seven years in prison for what she did to Samantha. "Seven years! She should've gotten a life sentence for doing what she did to that little girl!" I mumbled aloud. I put the car in gear and drove towards home.

Chapter 27

I returned home after four that evening, exhausted. I'd hoped to get some answers from Martha, but I wasn't any further than when I'd left the house. I had wasted my day driving back and forth, with what…five minutes of the woman's time? *What a joke*, I thought.

As I walked up the stone path to the porch, I noticed a large yellow envelope leaning against the door. I hurried up the creaky wooden steps, almost tripping as I raced for the package. I flipped it over in my hands, reading the return address. It was from the attorney that had sent the first few books of Tim's. I wondered if Michele had dropped off the package or if it had come straight here. I shook my head; it didn't matter who dropped it off.

I unlocked the front door and went inside. As I entered the kitchen, I had the envelope ripped open and was empting the contents on the table. Six more small books lay in front of me, along with a letter. I quickly snatched the letter up in my hand and opened it.

My dearest Carla,

Oh, how I love you so! I wish I didn't have to be sending you these books, but it was all I had left for you. I know you're probably confused by what's going on, but I assure you that when you read the very last book, you will understand my fullest intentions. I hope that you are well and that you are taking care of yourself. You deserve so much more than to sit and mourn my loss. Although, I would be just as devastated as you are now if anything ever happened to you.

You must learn to be strong because you really are! I know that you're hurt, but hurt doesn't have to last. You can be happy. I know I mentioned this in the first letter, but you must not close yourself off from the world outside.

You need to live your life, though it'll have to be without me, but I'll always be in your heart. When you feel the sun against your skin, it's me holding you, loving you for always.

I'll love you forever and always,

Tim

Once again, I was wiping the wetness from my cheeks. Reading the letter felt like he was still here with me. Like he was just leaving me a note before he went off to work, but I knew that wasn't true. I wasn't a fool to believe he hadn't died. I'd seen his body at the morgue. I had to, with

Veronica's help; identify his body, even though the cops knew it was Tim. Although with my approval, the Medical Examiner had to perform an autopsy to confirm the cause of death for their records.

I placed the letter against my chest, took in a deep, much-needed breath, and exhaled. I set the letter on the table and walked to the refrigerator. I hadn't eaten since yesterday, and my stomach growled at the thought of food.

I opened the freezer door, took out one of the many TV dinners I'd purchased at the store, and placed it in the microwave. My cooking days were nearing an end without anyone to cook for. I didn't care what I ate and where it came from. At this point, food was food as long as it filled my belly.

The microwave beeped. In one swift move, I opened the door of the microwave, grabbed the sides of the cardboard container, elbowed the door shut, and walked to the table. After setting my dinner down, I went and retrieved a fork.

I took a bite of my Salisbury steak and found it too hot. I set my fork with the meat on it back in the dish and reached for a book. I had to open all of them, to see the date where I'd left off before.

Thursday, 3/1/84

Today was pretty cool, when my friend Sean asked if I could come over after school so we could hang out and play on his Atari. I had never played an Atari before, so I was really hoping my mom would let me go to his house.

She said, "<u>Yes</u>!!!"

It was fun playing games on Sean's Atari. My favorite was Space Invaders! Sean's is Combat, but I don't really like those shooting games. Not when you have to shoot other people. I know it's all make-believe, but Space Invaders was much cooler! I can't wait to go back to his house and play the game again. Maybe for my birthday, I'll ask for one. Maybe not.

I really like my new mom and dad. I don't want them to not want me anymore because I ask for something. Besides, I am happy with what I have. It's definitely more than I've ever had before.

* * *

Wednesday, 3/21/84

Today is my new mom's birthday. We went out to eat after my counseling appointment.

We had Japanese food. It was so awesome to watch the man cook in front of us. He even made a choo-choo train from a stack of onions with what looked like smoke coming out the top. Then he flipped this egg in the air *without cracking it on his large spatula.*

It was so cool! My new dad got my mom a sparkly necklace for her birthday. I made her a card, which made me feel small; considering what my new dad had gotten her. But, after she opened the card, she seemed more thrilled with my present than his gift. That made me smile. My real dad, he didn't like the cards I made. He'd just open them, then say, "that's nice", and go back to watching whatever he was watching on TV.

I ate my dinner as I read Tim's journals. When I finished the first book, I threw my TV dinner away in the trash, and gathered the remaining books from the table. I *flicked* off the light in the kitchen and climbed the stairs to my bedroom. I set all the books down on the nightstand and went into the bathroom. The bathroom was large enough to fit both a shower and a whirlpool tub, and his and her sinks, something I had requested when the house was built.

I flipped the lever in the bathtub and turned on the hot water, testing it while adding cold water. I threw in some scented salts, and then lit the candles around the edge. Once the tub was half-full, I undressed and climbed inside.

The warmth surrounded my body, taking the achiness and stress away. I wasn't sure why I hadn't considered this weeks ago. Yes, I was mourning, but this felt like heaven to me. I leaned my head back against the cushioned pillow, closed my eyes, letting all my emotions slip away.

Forty-five minutes later, I climbed out of the tub, dried off, and slipped into my robe. After draining the tub and blowing out the candles, I threw on one of Tim's old T-shirts that I'd kept and slid under the covers. Once I was comfortable, I opened the book where I'd left off and started reading again.

An hour later, I tossed the book aside and grabbed another. It was past one in the morning when I started reading the last book that was sent to me. The last couple of books were dated in the year 1985, but the one I was now reading was in 1987. Tim had skipped a couple of years. Maybe the attorney had stuck the wrong book inside. That I didn't know, but it didn't seem to me that I'd missed anything from his life.

Midway through the last journal, the year changed to 1989, but that was only for a few pages before the year changed again, ending with 1993. A four-year gap and the year Tim turned eighteen. I hadn't met Tim until he was twenty so I was certain in the next set of books it would be when we got together.

I had a couple more pages to go before finishing the book. The first line intrigued me.

August 9th, 1993

I can't believe that I have a sister!
My parents hadn't even told me! I had
to find out by accident when I entered
the family room and heard them
discussing whether to tell me or not.
I've been in their house for ten years,
and this is the first I've heard anything

about having a sister. I'm not sure if she's my sister or a child that they had. But, then why wasn't she living with us? I want to ask them, but I don't want them to think I was eavesdropping on their conversation. Does it really matter? I just turned eighteen a week ago, and soon I will be going to college in Tallahassee, Florida. I think I have a right to know.

I turned the page, but there was nothing. *Had Tim known all along that he had a sister, but then that wouldn't make sense? Why would he have done a DNA test if he'd already known the truth?* I'd have to wait for the results to come back to get the answer, or… *Tim could've written it in his next journal?* The anticipation was killing me. It was like a mystery novel, but without the ending.

"Ugh!" I screeched. I had no idea when the results were going to show up or the next batch of journals. I'd have to keep myself busy in the meantime, which I had plenty of things to do. I still had to call the auto insurance company and send out his death certificate, and his life insurance policy still needed to be taken care of. There were a number of things to be done. First on that list would be to call Principal Steve Clapton at the school and go back to work. With everything else, what mattered most to me were my students. I needed to get back to them. To be surrounded by their laughter and silliness. Something I just now realized that I was missing.

I pushed the pile of books to Tim's side of the bed, clicked off the light and pulled the blankets under my chin.

Chapter 28

The following morning I was up and dressed by nine, seated at the table in the kitchen and writing a list of things that needed to be done:

* Call the school.
* Call auto insurance company first about my car and second to remove Tim's name from the policy.
* Call Life Insurance Company.
* Pay bills and look at checking account.
* Go to the bank and look at checking account.

I'd have to learn how to balance a checkbook, something Tim had always done. My checks from the school were direct deposit, so I didn't need to worry about that. Then I thought about his death certificate. *Where would I get something like that? Would the courts mail it to me, or was it something I had to take care of?* I thought. Maybe I'd give Pat a call and find out what I needed to do. I then added to the list:

* Call Pat Atkins.

* Call Attorney Robert Beckon.

I'd have to look up Attorney Beckon's name on the Internet, as I didn't have his number, and it wasn't on the envelope or letter he'd sent me. I dropped the pencil and grabbed the yellow envelope in front of me. I flipped it over and noticed there was no return address. In fact, this envelope was addressed to me directly, not Michele Channels, like the one before. It was odd to me, but I decided not to dwell on something as stupid as an address.

I glanced over my list again, checking to see if there was anything else to add. I didn't think so, and I stood up. I finished what was left of my coffee and placed my cup in the sink. I'd go to the bank first and then make all the phone calls once I returned home.

Ten minutes later, I parked the car at the bank and walked inside. After talking to one of the bank managers, which lasted about two minutes, only because I needed a death certificate to remove Tim's name from the account. Well, I knew what came next on the list. I climbed into the car and pulled my cell phone from my purse. I scanned the contacts until Pat's name appeared and hit the phone icon.

"Hello," Pat answered.

"Hey, Pat, it's Carla. Do you have a minute?"

"Yeah, sure, what's up?"

"Well, I'm sitting outside the bank, after talking to the manager; anyway, they say I need Tim's death certificate, but I'm not sure how to get it?" I said, running a hand through my hair as I talked.

"Didn't you get that after the memorial service?"

"I'm not sure?" I questioned. "I can't say my mind was in the right place. Even so, I wouldn't remember where I put the certificate."

"Well, in any case, I believe you have to contact the county or state vital records office. Hold on, I'll look it up for you," Pat replied. I could hear Pat tapping the keys on the keyboard, and then he said. "Okay, I found it." Pat rambled off the numbers.

"Thanks, Pat," I said.

"Call me if you need anything else."

"I will, thanks," I replied.

"Hey, Carla, before you go, how's everything going with you? Veronica and I haven't heard from you since the car accident. Is everything okay?"

"Yeah, I'm fine. You know, just busy with things," I replied, not knowing what else to say.

"Okay, well, let me know if you need anything," Pat stated, again.

"Sure, I will. Bye, Pat," I said and ended the call. I hadn't been much for conversation these days. I was the usual stay-around-the-house-and-mope kind of person. I didn't want to share that I'd been reading old journals of Tim's life. Then my friends would think I was falling back into depression, again. Just like a year ago.

I hadn't actually thought about what happened last year, at least not until now. It was after I'd lost the fourth baby from another miscarriage. I tried to return to my daily life, going to school, and teaching my students. It wasn't until school had ended at the end of May that I fell apart. I'd taken a bottle of Prozac hours before Tim was to come home from work. My mind whirred back to that day.

I swallowed the bottle of pills and lay on our bed, waiting. I'd tried to keep my eyes open for as long as I could. The scenery around me started fading away. I remember hearing his car door shut, and then the front door open. Tim started calling my name once he entered the house.

"Carla, I'm home," he had hollered.

I could hear him walking through the rooms downstairs, still calling out to me. I knew his next move would be to come upstairs.

"How about we go out to dinner tonight?" he had suggested. "I think it'd be good for you to get out of the house."

My body quivered as the boards on the stairs squeaked and groaned from his weight as he started up the stairs.

"Carla," he had said louder as he took the last step. He was now standing on the top of the landing.

I remembered his heavy footsteps as he made his way to our bedroom. "Carla, how about we go to a Jap..." he had stopped abruptly in the doorway, staring at my limp body on the bed.

I could see out the slits of my eyes and had tried to force my eyes all the way open, but they were too heavy. Suddenly, he appeared beside the bed, hovering over me. He then began shaking me and checking my pulse. I couldn't feel my arms, my fingers, the numbness moving down my body.

"Shit," he mumbled, then the sound of him pressing the musical keys on the phone next to the bed.

I recalled them not being rhythmic or calming in any way, as the darkness settled in.

"Please, you have to help her! She's not responding!" *he had screamed into the phone. "I found an empty bottle of Prozac next to the bed."*

I knew he'd try to save me, but I wasn't sure I wanted him to. However, if that was true, I'd taken the pills much sooner and not right before he came home from work. I'd figured two hours would've been more than enough time for the pills to do their job—to take my life. But, I had never expected him to come home early.

Still, time was of the essence. At that moment, I hoped the ambulance would take too long. That getting to the hospital would be too late.

I could feel my body drifting further away from me.

Then nothing...

I jumped from a tap on the car window, bringing me back to reality. I whipped my head towards the glass and saw a little old woman, smiling at me. I could see the woman's mouth moving, but couldn't hear what she was saying. I turned the key and fumbled for the button on the door; finally, the window went down.

"Are you all right, Miss?" the old lady asked.

I stared at the woman; she looked like the same lady I saw at the hospital before finding out that Mya and Tim had died. I blinked again, before answering, "I'm sorry, what did you say?"

"I asked if you were all right. You've been sitting in this car for over twenty minutes now," the old woman nodded, and then smiled.

"Twenty minutes?" I whispered. I must have blacked out when I ended the call with Pat.

"Yes, dear. I've been sitting in my car, waiting for my husband to come out of the bank. We pulled in shortly after you got back in your car. My car is right over there," the old lady pointed to a tan Cadillac, parked diagonally from my vehicle. "I saw you talking on the phone, and then you hung up and kind of just sat here, staring off. You didn't even move." The old lady shook her head. "I watched for quite a while, then decided to come over here and see if you were all right."

"Well, thank you for checking on me. I'm sorry I had you worried," I replied, with a smile.

The old lady patted my shoulder, "Ya' just take care of yourself now that you're all alone," the woman said as she strolled back towards her car.

I sat wide-eyed, trying to figure out how the woman knew I was now alone. The thought bothered me. When I snapped out of my daze, I looked over to where the old lady had said her car was.

It was gone.

Chapter 29

After leaving the bank, I drove towards home in deep thought. The weather had changed from a mild sunless day to rain, which fit the mood I was now in.

I still couldn't shake the weird encounter I had with the old lady. *How would she know that I'm alone now?* I kept replaying her words in my mind. Then, I remembered the old lady at the hospital. There was a woman there too. Could it have been the same woman?

I parked the car in my driveway and turned off the ignition. I thought back to the day Mya and Tim had died. The old lady had said to me, *"There, there, now, my sweet child. Things don't always seem as they are. It will be hard at first, but you'll work through them. Your daughter will live on, and so will your husband, Tim."* The woman had been right, but I didn't know how she could've known what had happened when the doctor hadn't told me yet? Then the woman had told me, *"It won't always be this hard. Follow your heart, and it will lead you to the very thing you've been wanting, my dear sweet child."*

I shook my head. "Who was this lady and how could she have known?" I mumbled aloud. I opened the car door, climbed out, and closed it behind me.

My neighbor, Deanna from across the street, hollered "hello" to me before I climbed the few stairs to my front door. I waved back to her, stuck the key in the lock, and went inside. I knew it seemed like I was avoiding her, but I just didn't feel like being social today.

As I walked into the kitchen—the same boring kitchen I'd been in so many times—I poured myself a glass of orange juice from the frig. I glanced around the room, noticing nothing different. I needed to get back to work before I lost my mind. Then a thought came to me. I'd been different this time. Sure, I'd spent a month in bed, but I was stronger now somehow. I'd actually made it through their deaths and was trying to move on.

"Yes, I did," I said to the empty room. I'd still have to take it one day at a time. A year ago, I wanted to die and actually tried to kill myself. The way I was missing Tim now; how could I have gone through with it back then? Did I not love him like I thought I did; like I do now?

Well, in all honesty, it didn't matter anymore. It was a year ago. Last year was a very tough time for me. After four miscarriages, Endometriosis, and then being told my chances were slim on ever having a baby, I overcame all the odds and had a baby girl, Mya, though she'd died a month later. *Yes, I'd been able to give my baby life! To fulfill my dream with my dear sweet Mya, and I will always love her, remember how she felt in my arms, and never ever forget how Tim had held her and kissed her tiny forehead! I AM NOT A FAILURE!*

I certainly wouldn't ever have the option again, now that I'd found out about the hysterectomy. My chances were definitely zero! Zilch! Was that what Tim was so afraid of?

But, the thing was, if I hadn't tried to kill myself, then I wouldn't be the person I was today. Then Mya wouldn't have been born, and maybe Tim would still be alive. All these things swam around in my mind. *The long and the short of it is*, I chuckled to myself, Tim had written that in his journal, and I had repeated it. I knew there was nothing I could do now. I couldn't change the past or the future. All I had now was to live in the present time and make the best of it. I needed to find out about the DNA results—period!

I took a sip of my juice, grabbed the handheld phone from the counter, and sat down at the table. I had several phones calls to make, and then I'd start putting away Tim's things that were still scattered on the table.

~ ~ ~ ~ ~

An hour later, I'd called and talked to Principal Clapton, letting him know that I would be returning to work the following Monday. I called both insurance companies; both telling me I needed Tim's death certificate to remove his name from the policy and to collect the life insurance.

I asked about my car and where it was being fixed. The woman on the phone said that a Veronica Rowan had made the call, since I was in the hospital recovering. I wrote down the business name, along with the phone number. I'd give them a call next.

I realized that Tim had taken care of more than just the banking. I'd never called any of these places before. Never had to take care of life's necessities. I hadn't been prepared for anything. I felt ashamed for not helping more, for not being a good wife to Tim. I really had been selfish.

Next, I had called the county vital records office and asked where I could get a copy of a death certificate. The man on the phone asked for the name and date of the person who was deceased. I heard him tapping away at the keys, and then he told me that they were filed at the county vital records office where he worked. I asked for the address and wrote it down.

Besides paying the bills, all I had left was to call Pat and Attorney Beckon. Beckon was at a court hearing so I left my name and phone number for him to call me back. I dialed Pat's number and waited for him to pick up.

"Carla, it's so nice to hear from you again," Pat answered.

"What do you mean, again?" I asked, confused.

"You called me a couple of hours ago. Don't you remember?"

"I did?" I was losing my mind. I tried to think back to earlier. Yes, I had been at the bank; I'd just climbed back into my car when I made the call. How could I have forgotten that I'd called him? But, what bothered me most was, I didn't recall what I'd talked to him about.

"Yeah, you called and asked me about where to get Tim's death certificate."

"Oh, yes, I remember now." That's how I'd known to call the county vital records office. I hoped I wasn't losing my mind now that Tim was gone. No, maybe I was just overwhelmed by everything I'd been doing today. Yes! That's what it was! I'd been making calls and remembering things from the past. Things I'd forgotten about, until today.

"Is everything all right?" Pat asked.

"What? Oh, yes; everything is fine. I've just been making all kinds of calls today and forgot that I'd called you earlier, that's all."

"Well, okay. If you need anything, don't hesitate to call me."

"Sure, I'll definitely call you if I need something, thanks," I said, before hanging up the phone and sitting back in the chair. I was feeling exhausted. I had no clue how much work was involved in making phone calls.

Twenty minutes later, I gathered my purse and went out the door. My first stop was the county vital records office and then back to the bank, before they closed for the day.

While I was at the county office, I paid for a copy of Mya's death certificate as well as ten copies of Tim's. Everyone I'd talked to today needed their own copy, plus the one I needed to keep for myself.

By the time I left the bank, finalizing my account, it was past five. I went home, made a hot cup of tea with honey, and curled up on the sofa, where I stayed the rest of the night.

Chapter 30

The next five days flew by. I had kept myself busy by storing Tim's things in the garage, cleaning the house, and doing the laundry. I got my car back and mailed out all of Tim's death certificates to the insurance companies.

When Monday arrived, I was up early and dressed for work. I was excited to see my students again. I also hoped that Samantha would be at school. I didn't know if she even lived in the same district as before. Was she even in the same town or state? Well, I'd find out as soon as I got to my classroom.

All of a sudden, I remembered Tim telling me that Michele Channels was taking care of Samantha. If I'd remembered it when Michele was at the house, I would've asked her about Samantha, but I hadn't.

I arrived an hour early, talked with Veronica, thanking her for all that she'd done, and then left the office. The walls along the hallway were covered with new drawings. I scanned over them as I made my way to my classroom. When I opened the door, I saw a huge sign hanging above the chalkboard saying, "Welcome back! Mrs. Michaels" with all the children's names written on it. I smiled as wetness filled my eyes. My students had missed me just as much as I had missed them.

I set my things on the desk and glanced around the room. I hadn't been back here since…since the day I'd went into labor. The day the doctor took all my chances of having a baby…away.

Of course, there wasn't any sign of blood or anything from that day almost two months ago. *And thank God, too. I wouldn't have been able to handle seeing any of that,* I thought.

I took out what I needed from my briefcase and placed it under the desk. A flicker of a memory came crashing back. I had tripped over the case, which caused me to fall and hit my head. I bent over and pushed it further under the desk, out of harm's way.

Today, I decided would be a fun day with my students. Since I'd been gone so long, I wanted to have an easy day and play games with the students, but still teach in the process.

I checked for any messages that might've been left on the desk phone—there weren't any. I sat down behind the desk and waited. I actually felt nervous which was not like me at all. Yes, I'd been gone for quite some time, but these were my students. Students I'd taught since last year. *But,* did it have to do with all of my students or just one in particular? Yes, I thought that must be it. I was worried about seeing Samantha. Maybe not worried, more like anxious, to see the little girl.

I snapped out of the trance I was in when a few of my students came into the room. None were Samantha. I said,

"Good morning," to the children as they placed their belongings at the back of the room and took their seats.

"Good morning, Mrs. Michaels," the three students replied, after they sat down.

"I'm so glad you're back," stated the boy named Brad.

"I'm glad to be back," I replied with a smile.

Ten minutes later, the rest of the children entered the classroom. I watched as each of them placed their things in the back and took their seats.

"Good morning class," I chimed.

"Good morning, Mrs. Michaels," the children sang in unison.

"I want to thank you all so much for making the sign for me. I love it very much! I missed all of you too."

I took attendance, but knew that everyone was here, except for Samantha. "Does anyone know where Samantha Berkley is?" I asked the class.

A girl named Amy McBeal raised her hand. "She doesn't go to this school anymore. My mommy said that she got taken away 'cause her mommy and daddy were mean to her."

"Oh," I replied. I shouldn't be shocked by what the girl had said, since I'd known myself that Samantha was being abused. "Well, thank you, for answering my question, Amy."

"You're welcome, Mrs. Michaels," Amy McBeal replied, smiling.

"Okay, students, today I thought we'd have a fun day." The children all cheered. "Does anyone have any suggestions on what we should do today?" I asked. Several students raised their hands. "Yes, Peter, what do you suggest we do?"

"I think we should play outside all day!" Half the students cheered.

"I know, Mrs. Michaels. We should all draw you pictures of how much we missed you," a girl named Bailey said.

Another student suggested a board game. Then other students started shouting out things they could all do.

"Quiet down, please," I demanded, raising my voice to let them know they were getting too loud. "Here's what I suggest. I want each of you to write down on a piece of paper what you'd like us to do today, along with your name. Then, I'll pick a student to pull from a hat, and that'll be what we do today. We'll play many different games. I can't promise you that we'll get a chance to do what each of you want, but the ones that don't get picked today, we'll pick one or two the following day, until everyone gets their choice, okay?"

The children all nodded in agreement. "Good," I smiled. "Now, write down your suggestion and fold the small piece of paper in half. Don't forget to write your name on the back so we know who has been picked. I will come around the room, and you'll drop your paper in the hat."

I walked to the back of the room and grabbed a top hat from the shelf. I started down each row, waiting for each student to finish, and then moved on until I had everyone's suggestion in the hat.

"Amy, please come up here and pick from the hat."

The little girl stood and made her way to the front of the class. She stuck her hand in the hat and pulled out a piece of paper, handing it to me.

"Thank you, Amy, you may sit down now." I unfolded the piece of paper. "Our first game is from Dominic. He would like to play, I Spy." A couple of the children moaned. "I think we should set up teams and keep score. The winning team will get ten extra minutes at recess."

"Cool," the children whispered.

I placed the students in two different groups. We played, I Spy, for an hour, and then picked from the hat again. My student Alisha wanted to have a jump-rope contest. I gathered up the students and led them to the gym in search of jump ropes.

The day moved along quickly, as we played games and laughed. I gleamed inside as I watched my students. I'd missed them so much and was glad to be back, but I was worried about Samantha. I missed the little girl. I wondered if I should find out where Michele lived and go see Samantha. I didn't think it was a bad idea and decided, why not?

The last bell of the day rang as my students gathered their things and stood by the door, waiting to be led out to the bus.

"Did you all have fun today?" I asked my class.

"Yes, Mrs. Michaels," they all chimed.

"Good. I'll be looking forward to seeing all your smiling faces tomorrow for some more fun." The children cheered. "Okay, if we're all ready, let's go."

I led the children down the hall and out the door to where the buses were lined up. I waved to each of the children as they climbed the steps of the bus and took their seats.

"Carla, how are you doing?" Principal Steve Clapton asked.

"I'm good, thank you for asking," I replied.

"How does it feel to be back to work?"

"It feels great!"

"Good. That's good to hear." Principal Clapton replied.

I hadn't really noticed his appearance before. He wasn't any taller than five-ten at the most and had dark brown hair that curled at the ends. I watched as he rubbed his hands together and how large they were. I wasn't sure if he was nervous about something. I didn't really care, but he shouldn't be nervous around me—we'd known each other for years. Then it dawned on me that some of the teachers in the staff cafeteria today were acting awkward around me too. Well, to think of it, I'd probably act the same way if someone I knew had lost both her baby and her husband at the same time, the same day. I shook the thought away.

"Is there something I can help you with?" I asked.

"No, no. Just wanted to see how you're doing," he replied, almost in a sympathetic voice.

"Okay. Well, I have some things to finish up. See you tomorrow," I said, as I walked away, not waiting for him to respond.

Once back in my classroom, I gathered my things, placed them on the desk, and looked around the room. I put the strap of my purse on my shoulder and walked out of the room, closing the door behind me.

On my way out, I stopped at the front office. Veronica wasn't sitting at her desk, nor was she anywhere in the room. I turned, walked out the main door, and towards my car, which I'd called and taken a taxi to go get on Saturday.

I placed my things on the backseat and sat behind the wheel. I drove home, hoping to find more of Tim's journals at the door. No such luck. I parked the car, climbed out, and after gathering my things, I went inside.

The silence that I'd known for years was different than before. Maybe because back then I knew Tim would be arriving home soon, but not now, not anymore. I set down my briefcase and purse on the bench by the door and walked into the kitchen. I found the envelope that Michele had brought over and read the address on the front. There was no talking me out of going to Michele's house. Besides, what would it hurt by going? Samantha was a student of mine, plain and simple! Whatever differences Michele and I were having, we'd have to put them on the back-burner for Samantha's sake. I changed into comfortable shoes, grabbed my purse, and headed out the door.

Chapter 31

Ten minutes later, I turned onto the street where Michele Channels lived. I coasted down the road until I saw the house number 2371. I pulled into the driveway and shut off the car. I sat behind the wheel, staring out the windshield. *Well, it's too late to turn back now,* I thought.

I grabbed my purse from the front seat and opened the door. I straightened my posture as I stood, held my head up high, and walked to the front door. I took in a deep breath and rang the doorbell.

"Coming," a woman hollered, probably Michele.

I wiped my palm against my pant leg as I waited patiently for Michele to answer the door. I swallowed when the door creaked open, saw no one, and looked down. A small boy stood inside the doorway; a wide and toothless grin spread across his face.

"Hello," I said.

"Hi, I'm Robby. Are you here to see Michele?" Robby asked, still smiling at me.

"Ah, yes. Yes, I am," I replied. "No, actually…" I paused. "I'm looking for a girl named Samantha."

"Which Samantha? We have two here by that name."

"Oh, well, her name is Samantha Berkley."

"Yeah, she's here. You want me to go get her?" Robby asked.

I smiled, "Yes, that would be nice, thank you."

"Robby, who's at the door?" Michele asked, as she walked down the hall, making her way to the front door.

"I don't know her name. I forgot to ask."

"Remember? I told you not to open the door, unless I tell you to."

"Sorry, I keep forgetting," Robby mumbled, then turned from the door and ran up the stairs.

Michele opened the door wider. "Sorry about that..." Michele stopped in mid-sentence. "Carla, what are you doing here?" she asked, looking confused.

"Hi, I, ah... I was hoping I could see Samantha, Samantha Berkley."

"What is it you need to see her about?" Michele questioned.

"She's a student of mine or was a student of mine," I explained, almost in a whisper. "Is there a problem with me seeing her?"

"No," Michele replied. "I guess not, you were her teacher, after all."

I painted a smile on my face, hoping Michele couldn't tell how fake it was.

"About the other day. I...I want to say I'm sorry for putting my nose into your and Tim's past affairs," Michele squeaked.

"Oh, well, all's forgotten," I replied, which wasn't a total lie.

"That's good to hear. I'm sorry, please come in." Michele motioned me to step inside, and then closed the door. "Sorry about the mess. I have seven children here right now, and the rooms seem to get a little messier with their things. I keep telling them to put their toys back in their rooms, or I'm going to throw them all away. You know how youngsters are," Michele stated in one breath.

I nodded with a smile, though; I didn't have any troubles with my students listening to the rules. Maybe, Michele was too nice of a person, and let them do what they wanted.

"Come, please have a seat, and I'll go get Samantha." Before Michele placed her foot on the first step, Samantha came prancing down the stairs. "I was just coming up to get you," Michele said.

"Robby said I have a visitor. Is it Mr. Michaels, again?" Samantha asked, smiling. "I haven't seen him in a long time. I hope it's Mr. Michaels."

Confusion swept through me when I heard the words Samantha had just said. Why had Tim come here to see Samantha? How often did he come here? Maybe it had something to do with the case, and he had to ask her questions. *Yeah, that was possible,* I thought, *but why hadn't he said anything to me?* Not that he had to tell me everything. It made sense because this was a case he was working on, and he had to keep things confidential. Still, the thought of him coming here bothered me. I didn't know why, and then remembered the DNA test. Did he already know the truth and was coming here to see her other than for work? Yes, that was a possibility too.

"Mrs. Michaels, you came to see me!" Samantha cheered.

I rose from my seat on the sofa as Samantha ran into my arms. I hugged her tight and then held her out at arms-length. "You look so happy, Samantha, and you got your cast off too."

"I missed you so much, Mrs. Michaels. Where have you been? Where's Mr. Michaels at?"

I sucked in a breath and looked up at Michele. Michele mouthed the words, "I'm sorry. I couldn't tell her".

I nodded in response. "Is it all right if we go for a walk?" I asked Michele.

"Sure, that'll be fine," said Michele, before turning and leaving the room.

I placed my arm on the back of Samantha's shoulder as I opened the door and we went outside.

"I'm so glad you came to see me Mrs. Michaels." Samantha fell into step with me, and slid her small hand into mine.

I smiled at the feel of the little girl's hand in mine. "Well, I just returned to the school today, and I didn't see you. Amy McBeal said she heard that you were going to a different school."

"Ya', but I don't like my teacher," Samantha replied with a frown.

"Well…" I wasn't sure how to answer. "Sometimes, there'll be teachers we like better than others, but I'm sure you don't dislike your teacher."

Samantha's mouth twisted from side-to-side, as she thought about what I had said. "No, I guess I don't dislike Ms. Rainfall, but she ain't as nice as you, Mrs. Michaels. I'd rather have you as my teacher," Samantha said.

"Let me see what I can do about that once we get back to the house, okay?"

Samantha nodded and smiled, "Okay."

I saw that Samantha had lost another tooth when she smiled up at me. "So," I cleared my throat. "So, Mr. Michaels was coming here to see you?"

Samantha nodded.

"May I ask, what the two of you talked about?"

"You can ask me anything you want, Mrs. Michaels."

"So, what was it Mr. Michaels came to see you about?"

"Sometimes, he asked me questions about my mommy."

"What kind of questions?" I pressed.

"Like, where I was born, and if I had ever met my mommy's parents. I told him I didn't know. My mommy and daddy never told me anything about their families. We never went to other people's houses."

"Oh, anything else he might have asked you?"

Samantha shrugged her shoulders, "I don't remember. Why hasn't Mr. Michaels come to see me? Did I do something wrong?"

I stopped, knelt down, and looked Samantha in the eyes. "No! Of course, you didn't do anything wrong." I scanned the scenery, looking for a place we could sit, and I could tell Samantha what had happened to Tim. "Let's go sit under that tree so I can talk to you."

Samantha sat Indian style in front of me, her hands folded in her lap, a smile on her face.

I looked at this fragile child in front of me; looking for any significance, she may be Tim's niece. Her eyes were blue, like Tim's. She had dirty blonde hair; Tim's was brown like mine. Nothing about this girl told me that Tim was related to her, but that didn't mean anything. Kids were born all the time and didn't always look like their parents or relatives. This could be one of those times.

"So, why hasn't Mr. Michaels come to see me?"

I reached out my hand, smoothed my fingers along Samantha's cheek. "I'm sorry, sweetie, but Mr. Michaels, he…he died sweetie. He's in heaven now."

"What's heaven?" Samantha asked. "Did he move without telling me?"

Part of me wanted to smile at her words, but the other part knew I had to explain what heaven was and why Tim had gone there. "Mr. Michaels didn't move, sweetie. Heaven is a place people go when they… when they die. I'm sorry sweetie, but Tim was killed last month. Do you know what killed means?" I asked.

Samantha nodded, "It means he's dead and he ain't coming back, right? He didn't even say goodbye to me," she said. "Why didn't he say goodbye?" Samantha blinked, then blinked again. She opened her mouth to speak again, but nothing came out. A tear escaped when she squeezed her eyes together and slid down her face. I wiped the tear away, wrapped my arms around the little girl, and let her cry. I wanted to tell her that he never said goodbye to me either.

After talking with Samantha, I took her back to the house and promised to come see her as much as I could. I also talked to Michele about having Samantha return to her old school, which Michele had agreed without a dispute.

I returned home an hour later, and to my surprise there was an envelope from Genetic DNA Laboratories, Inc. in the mailbox. I ripped open the tab and reached inside, pulling out several papers:

Dear Mrs. Michaels:

Per your request, our laboratory ran the samples you have sent us. Although, the results are enclosed, there still seem to be inconclusive results. We will keep your file active for 60 days, and then it'll be closed and filed away.

Any questions or concerns, please don't hesitate to call my number directly.

Sincerely,
Mrs. Barbara Collins
Genetic DNA Laboratories, Inc.
1-700-555-5555 Ext. 218

I swallowed, moved the paper to the back, and scanned the results. Was I right? Was Tim Samantha's uncle? Though, Barbara stated that the results were *still inconclusive*. What was I missing? Whose DNA did they need to make this test accurate? Maybe I needed to call this Barbara woman and ask her these questions? I didn't understand the results, but somehow, they were related, but in what way?

I closed the lid to the mailbox and trudged up the walk. I turned the key, opened the front door, and went inside. I was nowhere closer to the truth than I was last week.

I set my purse on the table, along with the mail I'd brought in, and slumped down in the chair in the kitchen, feeling exhausted. My head was pounding so I placed my head on my arm that was lying across the top of the table. I just needed to clear my mind and think about what I should do.

After several minutes, I stood and went to the refrigerator. I hadn't been eating well and figured my sugar was probably low, which was making me tired all the time. I grabbed a TV dinner from the freezer, set it in the microwave, and leaned against the counter. When the microwave *chimed*, I removed the container and placed it on a plate. I grabbed a fork and made my way to Tim's office, off the foyer. I moved the chair out with my foot and sat down.

Tim had always been organized when it came to paperwork. There wasn't a cluttered spot anywhere on the Victorian desk. I turned the small knob at the base of the lamp; light cascaded across the desk.

I moved the mouse, but the computer didn't make a sound. I reached behind the monitor, pushed the button in, and waited for the sound of the computer to boot up. The monitor slowly came to life, and then flicked to a black screen with the word *password* and a box beside it. My forehead wrinkled in confusion. *When had he put a password on the computer? Had there always been one, and I didn't remember?* Yes, I was sure that was it.

Lately, I'd forgotten quite a bit about the things I'd done in the past. I'd hit my head in the accident. Yes, that had to be why. No, wait. I'd hit my head when I was having contractions, but that was months ago. Could that have caused me to forget things now? I wasn't sure, but would worry about it later, if things continued to get worse.

I typed in a couple different words, but kept getting the words "try again". I tried to think what Tim would've used as a password, but none of those worked either. I looked around the desk for a sticky note or any kind of paper with the password on it. The desk was way too neat and clean, and a piece of paper like that would definitely stick out like a sore thumb.

I opened the top drawer, searched around, looked inside books, but still nothing. Maybe this was a test of some sort. I had to sit and think what Tim would use. I tried several more words, but still ended up with an *error*. I decided to eat my dinner before it got too cold, but at the same time, I kept thinking about the password.

I took a bite of my food and scanned the room. My eyes searched the bookshelf in front of me. Tim loved to collect old books. Most of the books were his law books, but he had after several years of marriage, shown an interest in old novels about history. I figured there had to be at least fifty books lined up on the shelves, but only one caught my eye.

I stood, walked over to the shelf, and with the tips of my toes, reached up as far as I could for the book. The long nails of my slender fingers touched the binding, but I wasn't able to pull the book out.

I went back to the desk, wheeled the chair over and cautiously climbed onto the padded seat. The wheels on the chair started to roll away from the wall. I quickly grabbed at the wooden shelf as the chair moved further away. In that split second, I had my fingers stretched out and grabbed the wood, pinching it like a white-headed pimple. With all my strength, I pulled myself towards the bookshelf, quickly grabbed hold of the book, and leaped out of the chair.

Placing a hand on my chest, I took several steady breaths to slow my speeding heart. I grabbed the chair, guided it back to the other side of the desk, and sat down. I pushed my plate aside, set the book down, and opened it.

It looked to me to be another one of Tim's journals. The date written was *eight* years ago. There was no way I could remember much of anything from 2007, more or less what happened yesterday. I guided my finger down the page as I began to read:

May 6th, 2007

Carla is having difficulty getting pregnant. Two months ago, she lost our first child. I don't know whether it was a girl or a boy. The doctor had said there would've been no way of knowing since she was only seven weeks along.

She says she wants to keep trying, but I don't want to hurt her. I don't want to cause her to have another miscarriage.

Well, I don't think it's my fault she lost the baby, but I'd rather take the blame than let her carry the guilt, when in all honesty, it's not her fault, either. I've tried many times to tell her that, and the doctor confirmed it as well.

Carla tends to hold her feelings inside her and then bam!—she explodes into a million pieces, with a million things coming out that happened months or even years ago. I've tried to tell her to open up and talk to me. That I won't judge her in any way, and that I love her no matter what.

I hear her crying in the bathroom most nights, but she comes out of the room as if all is well. The most I can do is listen to her. Be there when she needs to talk. Give her that shoulder to cry on when she needs it. Continue to tell her she's not alone and that I'll always be here for her. That's all I can do...

I wiped the tears from my eye. I remembered that day as if it was yesterday, the sadness of losing my first baby.

I shouldn't be shocked that Tim had written about the pregnancies, but I was. I hadn't realized how much he had really loved and cared for me. Had I been so consumed with myself to not see it? To not feel his love for me? I hadn't even considered how Tim had felt about me losing the babies. How it broke his heart, like it broke mine. And why wouldn't it? He was just as human as I was; he hurt when I hurt.

I spotted a framed picture of us together at the far corner of the desk. I reached out and grabbed the frame, bringing it closer to me. It was a photo of us on our wedding day. I studied every detail of Tim. The way his lip curled when he smiled, and one single dimple in his right cheek. Then it hit me; Samantha had the same dimple every time she smiled.

Chapter 32

I thought of Samantha from earlier. Yes! She definitely had the same dimple in her cheek. *But,* what did that mean, exactly? It had never occurred to me that Tim would be the girl's father. No! Tim wouldn't cheat on me. He wouldn't have had an affair with Martha Berkley, or Kathy Sonnets, of all people. The thought of it made me nauseous.

Samantha was seven years old or she would be seven. Why would he sleep with someone else when we were trying to have a baby? Had I pushed him away from me? No! I knew I hadn't done that. I wanted to keep trying for a baby. Did Tim want to have a child so desperately that he just couldn't wait for us to have one of our own, or did he believe that I would never be able to give him a baby? He would have told me something that important, wouldn't he?

My head was spinning in circles. These past couple of weeks were too much for me. Why had it taken Tim to die for me to find out all of this? All these hidden secrets. Had I really been this clueless about my own husband? I set the frame down on the desk and picked up the journal. Maybe Tim had written about the things I was wondering about.

May 16th, 2006

Carla's been lying around in bed, not wanting to get up. I think she suffers from depression, but I'm not sure how to help her. She wants to try to have another baby, but I think it's too soon for us to try. I've tried telling her that, but she seems very determined to have a baby.

I'm not saying I don't want one, but I feel she means more to me than having something hurt her, or worse, kill her. I know we'll try again, but it's only been ten days. The doctor said to, at least, wait six weeks. Maybe I'll just let her have some time to mend, and when she's ready to get out of bed, then we'll go from there.

* * *

June 18th, 2006

Carla and I have talked and we're going to try again. The doctor told her that he wasn't going to run any tests unless she continues to have miscarriages. Something about the fetus being rejected, and it's the body's way of emptying the bad cells. I guess I understand what he's saying. The doctor thinks we should continue trying to have a baby and see what happens.

* * *

August 29th, 2006

Well, Carla's pregnant. I should sound more thrilled as I write this, but I just don't want to get my hopes up and she loses the baby, again.

She seems to be handling it well. She seems more excited, energetic. Carla smiles every time we're around each other. She's happy, which makes me happy.

I was worried when she was lying in bed after the first miscarriage. I wish her mom were still alive to be here with her, to help her. I was thankful, Carla's friend, Ashley from Ohio came to visit and get her out of bed. Ashley even got her to sit outside a few times, and to actually eat dinner with us. I thought she was getting better until Ashley had to leave, then she crawled back into bed, as if nothing had happened.

I'm not sure what I can do to help her. I love her so much, but my heart is breaking inside. I want to talk to her about adopting a baby or a child of *any age, but I don't think she'll agree with it.*

I'm just praying this baby survives. I don't think Carla can handle losing another baby.

I swallowed hard, forcing the bile back down my throat. If I'd let Tim talk to me about adopting a baby, then he'd still be alive. Maybe? I knew that was a lie, he would've still been at the courthouse at the same time, on the same day, with some other case. I didn't believe that time and fate would've been altered in such a way that Tim would be alive. What did I know anyway—I wasn't a psychic. I wasn't anyone special! Actually, yes, in Tim's journals I was. Apparently, I was everything to him, and I never saw it, or never tried to see it.

September 22nd, 2007

She lost the baby!

I'm not sure how much longer I can hide my grief from her. I want to be the strong one—I have to be. She's been lying in bed again. I'm not sure what else I can do for her. How to help her...

I came home from work two weeks after she'd lost the baby and found her in a lot of pain. I took her right away to the hospital, but it wasn't until the entire tests came back negative that the doctor suggested she have a Laparoscopy.

The doctor told us, he has no doubt she has Endometriosis; a disease that causes extreme abdominal pain, painful intercourse, and miscarriages.

Before the doctor took her into surgery, I talked to him in private. I asked him to remove some of Carla's eggs and have them frozen, just in case something went wrong. The doctor assured me nothing would go wrong. She shouldn't have any further problems once the surgery was preformed.

I didn't want to take any chances. I will make sure she has a baby of her own.

After reading what Tim asked the doctor to do, I closed the book. I couldn't make myself read anymore. I just went to bed.

Chapter 33

The following morning, I woke before the alarm. In fact, I'd been awake for nearly two hours, staring up at the ceiling. Thinking about all the things, I'd found out in the past couple of weeks. Tim's journals, the hysterectomy I'd been given, Tim being abused by his own father and then was adopted, Tim having a sister, (which I wasn't certain about) and now just learning he'd had my eggs frozen.

If the DNA test was correct, then, yes, Tim and Martha Berkley have a connection to one another. I made a mental note to call Barbara Collins on my lunch break, though I was uncertain if I could wholeheartedly rely on my memory. With that thought in mind, I threw back the covers and climbed out of bed.

I scooped three teaspoons of sugar in my coffee, stirred, and went to the office to retrieve Tim's journal from last night. No, I knew I wasn't going to sit down and read more of the book, right now. I'd wait until I got home from work to do that. No sense starting the day off with more surprises, more untold and hidden secrets. I climbed the stairs and went into the bedroom to get ready for work.

After a nice hot shower, which I badly needed to clear my mind, I dressed and went back downstairs. I poured myself another cup, sat down at the table, and scanned through the pages of the DNA. I'd need to take these with me so I could ask this Barbara woman the right questions. I gulped down the last of my coffee, placed the cup in the sink, and walked out the door.

~ ~ ~ ~ ~

At eleven thirty, I sat at my desk, papers in front of me, and the phone in my right hand. I punched the numbers in and waited for someone to answer. An automated voice came on the line and asked for the extension I wanted to reach. I tapped two-eighteen into the number pad.

The line began to ring. Part of me wanted to hang-up, but the other part wanted to know the truth. I couldn't continue with my life, without knowing all of Tim's secrets. It was like getting a second chance to know my husband, my real husband. The one who was supposed to be honest with me in our marriage. Weren't those words in our vows? Honesty? I couldn't remember exactly from ten years ago.

Three rings, then four.

Was I going to have to leave a message? I didn't want to, but if I wanted answers, I'd have to and the woman would call me back. Five rings.

"Hello, Genetic Laboratories. How may I help you?"

My mouth went dry. I had to say something before the woman hung up on me. "Is…Is this Barbara Collins?" I choked out.

"Yes, this is she. Is there something I can help you with?" The woman's voice sounded sweet, caring. Like a mother comforting a child who'd been hurt falling off their bike.

"Hi, yes, my name is Carla Michaels. I sent you some samples a week ago, and I received the results back, but I have some questions," I replied, in my teacher voice.

"Oh, yes. I remember the name. What questions can I help you with?"

"Well, I don't know much about DNA so first, if you can tell me about the different numbers, and what they mean?"

"Let me bring the results up on my computer here, just one second." The tapping of the keyboard filled the line as I waited for Barbara to speak again. "Here we go. Okay, so the last test that we did shows that Tim Michaels *is not* excluded from being the father of the child of Samantha Berkley."

I gasped, "Father?"

"Yes," Barbara replied. "Samantha and Tim have the same numbers, which gives the test a probability of 99.99%. As for Martha Berkley, the numbers don't match-up. Martha and the child have only two numbers that match, which could mean they are related, but not necessarily."

"So, you're telling me that Tim is the biological father of Samantha, but Martha isn't her biological mother."

"Yes, ma'am, that's what I'm telling you. There could be some relation between the two, but not as mother and father. Martha has more similarities to Tim than the child. Which could mean…"

"Tim and Martha are brother and sister," I interrupted.

"That could be a possibility. If Martha were the child's mother, they'd have the same numbers Tim has with the child, but she doesn't."

"Can you do a test to see if they're brother and sister?"

"Yes, I can do that. I'll need you to provide me with a sample of Martha's saliva and Tim's if you can."

"Oh," I whispered. "Tim passed away last month, but I can send you some more samples of his hair. Will that work?"

"Oh, I'm so sorry for your loss. Yes, we can use his hair as DNA. Can you gather some samples from Martha?"

"Yeah, I can get you a sample. It'll take me some time, but I can get it for you."

"Great! Oh, before I forget. You should send your sample in as well. It wouldn't hurt to check your DNA with all three."

I blinked, "Sure, I guess I can give you a sample."

"Great! Are there any other questions?"

My mind was blank. Had I asked Barbara all the questions I wanted to? I couldn't remember. I was still in shock that Tim was Samantha's father. It didn't even dawn on me if I'd been rude when I responded "no", and without thinking, hung up the phone.

My mind whirled with this new information that I was startled when the door to the classroom swung open and my students poured into the room. I'd have to push my thoughts away until school was over and then figure out what I needed to do.

Chapter 34

The dashboard of my car read 4:05 p.m., when I pulled into my driveway. I'd been trying to come up with a plan. I'd have to either take a day off of work, or drive down first thing Saturday morning, to get a sample of Martha's saliva. The question was, how? I didn't think Martha would willingly give me a sample. I'd have to come up with something to convince her to do it. I could just tell her the truth. Hell, I'd already mentioned that Tim and her *could be* siblings. I showed her the papers, though; Martha didn't want to believe it. Didn't want to hear what I had to say. Did I have the strength to go back down there and see her again? Martha had been mean—cruel even. Yes, I had to do this. I had to get to the bottom of this, once and for all.

I climbed out of the car and closed the door. I started to walk towards the house when I heard a familiar voice calling my name.

"Carla," the female voice shouted.

I turned to see my neighbor Deanna Iris waving me over. Wait, no, her last name wasn't Iris anymore. She'd married her neighbor, Brice Augustin. I had only talked to Brice a few times, but I'd never forget his French accent.

I looked both ways before crossing the street, making my way to Deanna's driveway.

"Hey, how have you been?" Deanna asked.

I faked a smile, not wanting to talk about how I was doing personally. "I'm doing good, and yourself?"

"Great! I'm almost finished with my fifth novel, but I think I'm going to take a small break for a while. Brice wants to take a few weeks and travel to all the New England states this summer. Maybe I'll get some good ideas from the trip for my next book," Deanna said in one long breath.

"Wow, that sounds amazing." I wish I'd pretended not to notice my neighbor and kept on walking. I wasn't in the mood to talk, which wasn't anything new. Besides, Deanna was always so... so chipper. Although, I'd be the same after what Deanna had been through; I'd be a different person too.

The story I heard from Deanna herself was that she had moved back to her hometown with her son, Brent. Her sister Shelia had offered to pick-up Brent from school, but they'd gotten into an accident and were both hospitalized. Shelia was in a coma. To make a long story short, Deanna had some past secrets surface that nearly got her killed!

"Sorry, you look like you have a lot on your mind. You know I'm here if you ever want to talk," Deanna replied.

"What? No, I'm good. Really, I am. Just been busy now that I went back to work, trying to get my life situated the best I can," I replied, almost wishing I'd shut my mouth. Sometimes when I got all built-up inside, words would just pour out of me. I tried many times to control myself and not spill my guts on everything that was bothering me. Tim always used to tell me that I could talk to him and not hold things inside. That he wouldn't judge me. He'd only listen.

"Sure, I know what you're talking about. I didn't think I'd ever be able to start a new life with Brice, but I just put one foot in front of the other and kept on moving."

"Sounds like good therapy."

"It is, when you put your mind to it," Deanna said, reaching her hand out and patting my arm. "I know what it's like to lose a child, but I wouldn't change a thing I have now. I have a great man who loves me to the moon and back."

I nodded as Deanna kept on talking. This wasn't a conversation I wanted to have right now. Not after everything I'd found out.

"Brice has been working long hours at the Lab these past few weeks. I swear, every animal has to be tested, and their DNA stored for future testing."

"Did you say that Brice does DNA testing?" I perked up, moved closer, not wanting to miss a word Deanna was saying.

"Yeah, he works with animals. He needs to check their DNA samples with the other species."

"Has he ever tested human DNA samples?" I asked, waiting anxiously for a reply.

Deanna nodded, "Yes, he has. Why do you ask?"

I shrugged my shoulders, "Just wanted to know."

Deanna eyed me closely. "If you want something tested, he'll do it for you," Deanna whispered.

I took a step back, my eyes wide, shaking my head as I spoke, "I didn't indicate that I needed something tested," I replied defensively.

"Oh, well, I'm sorry for assuming you did. I just thought… I mean you sounded interested in what my husband does for a living. My mistake," Deanna stated, then turned and walked back up the drive and into the open garage.

Apparently, I had hit a sore spot. I stood still as I watched the garage door begin to close. I let out a deep breath, turned, and crossed the street.

Once inside, I placed my things on the kitchen table, and went into the office. I moved the chair out and sat down, as soon as I touched the mouse the monitor lit-up. The small box remained, waiting for the secret password.

"Think Carla. What would Tim use?" I thought aloud. My fingers magically started moving over the keys without even knowing I was doing it. I typed in the letters S A M A N T H A and hit enter. The screen disappeared.

Bingo, I had actually typed in the correct word. Although, I wasn't sure how I knew what the password was, and I wasn't going to sit here figuring it out either, or why it was Samantha's name.

A picture of us on our wedding day appeared. Tim had actually saved it on his desktop. Three seconds later, another picture appeared. It was like watching a slideshow of our life together.

A tear rolled down my face as I watched the years with Tim pass in front of me. God, I missed him so much! What I wouldn't do to have him back again! To hold him one more time. To love him the way he should've been loved when he was here. I knew I couldn't bring him back, but I would never forget him; no matter how many secrets he held from me. I loved him with all my heart.

I wiped the tears away and clicked on the Internet icon. I typed the word DNA in the browser and hit enter. I sat there reading about test results, siblings, and parents; everything I could find about DNA. I even looked up what a person needed to gather for a DNA test. I'd need to go to the store and get a couple of home-tests, so I could get saliva samples. Although, I wished I could talk to Brice about all of this. Maybe he'd know what to do, but I wasn't sure if I wanted the whole neighborhood to know what was going on. Not that Brice or Deanna would tell the neighbors. I hadn't heard about Deanna's past from other people; I had only heard about it from Deanna.

I honestly didn't know what to do. I could start by trying to find more of Tim's hair, or even a toothbrush, or a razor. I'd stop by the store tomorrow and buy a couple testing boxes, then go from there.

Chapter 35

The next morning, I woke before the alarm. I showered, dressed, and was sitting in the kitchen drinking my third cup of coffee, when there was a knock at the front door.

My eyes automatically looked at the clock on the wall, trying to fathom why someone would be knocking on my door at six in the morning.

I set down my cup, stood, and walked to the door. I flipped the deadbolt and turned the knob. I was a little surprised to find Deanna standing on my porch.

"Hi, Carla. I wanted to apologize for my behavior yesterday. I shouldn't have said what I did. I'm sorry," Deanna said, looking sympathetic.

"Oh, well, you didn't have to come over and apologize for that," I replied, waving my hand in the air.

"No, really; I'm sorry. I should be more understanding. What, with everything you've been going through and all. Hell, I've been there myself." Deanna could see that I looked confused.

My eyes hardened, making the skin on my forehead wrinkle. *What was Deanna's point? Does she know what I found out? Does she know that Tim might have had an affair?*

"Carla, may I come in for a minute?"

I moved aside without hesitation. Deanna walked past me and went into the kitchen. I felt as if I were in a dream, moving along steadily and smoothly, almost like a ghost.

I closed the door and followed Deanna into the room. My neighbor pulled a chair out and sat down.

"Would you like a cup of coffee?" I asked.

"Yes, I'd love a cup; thank you for asking."

I poured her a cup and placed it down in front of her, along with some sugar. She was like me; we weren't cream-in-our-coffee lovers. "So, what brings you over to my house at the crack of dawn? I mean you said you wanted to apologize, which you did, but I believe there's more to you coming than just that," I said as I took my seat.

Deanna stirred her coffee after adding sugar. "Tim was over to see Brice before he was killed. I don't know the whole story, but I overheard Tim asking Brice questions about a DNA test. Something about what he would need to get one done and where he could go to have it tested. Brice didn't know I was listening, and I didn't ask him any questions about what they talked about," Deanna assured. "I mean, if Brice wanted me to know he would've told me, ya' know? So, I didn't ask. In fact, I somewhat forgot about the whole thing when I found out Tim had died. Well, until yesterday," Deanna looked up from her cup and met my eyes.

I wanted to tell her; I needed to tell her everything that I knew, what I had found out. I believed that I could trust Deanna, right? Look at what she'd gone through two years ago with her life. Finding out the truth about her childhood could've gotten her killed! She even told me that her daughter was not forgotten, not even once in her life. Yes, I could trust this woman in front of me. I could tell her all of the secrets I'd found out in these past two weeks. I swallowed and opened up to Deanna, telling her everything I knew.

~ ~ ~ ~ ~

When I finished, I glanced up at the clock, noticing the time. I still had over an hour before I needed to be at the school.

"I'm…I'm so sorry. I'm not sure what to say. Do you think this girl is really Tim's daughter? You think he had an affair? God, I'm so sorry. You must be going crazy with all of this," Deanna blew out a breath.

"I don't know what to think," I replied. "All I know is that I need to find a way to get this Martha woman's DNA, in order to do the test. Barbara even suggested that I send mine in as well."

"Why?"

"Not sure. Maybe to get me excluded from the test." I shrugged my shoulders.

"Would you mind if I have Brice take a look at the results? Maybe he could explain them better to you."

"Yeah, I guess, but Barbara already confirmed that Tim is Samantha's father. What would Brice find that Barbara didn't already tell me?"

"Hopefully something other than Tim getting another woman pregnant!" Deanna exclaimed.

"Isn't that the truth? Thanks, Deanna, for listening and wanting to help."

"If I know anything, it's definitely about people hiding secrets."

"How is Kimberly doing by the way?" I asked.

"She's doing great! She moved out to this area last year. She works in the ICU at Silver Cross Hospital," Deanna replied with a smile.

"That's wonderful news, Deanna. I'm so glad that everything worked out the way it did."

"Me too. I guess sometimes we need to go through these rough patches to get to where we are today."

I nodded. *Was this a rough patch? Was I going to get to the bottom of this? Yes, of course, I'd find out the answers. I wasn't going to rest until I did. Good or bad, I needed to get to the truth of this mess that Tim had made.*

~ ~ ~ ~ ~

Deanna had left shortly after our talk, and now I was heading to work. I'd given her a copy of the test results and kept the originals for myself. Deanna also said she'd give me a call after she talked to Brice.

Last night, I had made the decision before I fell asleep to drive down and pay a visit to Martha on Saturday. Now, I just had to make it through the rest of the week.

I arrived at the school ten minutes later and parked the car. I stopped at the office to see Veronica, but she wasn't at her desk so I grabbed my mail from the box and went to my classroom.

Fifteen minutes later, the students arrived. I frowned when I didn't see Samantha. Michele had told me that

Samantha would be coming back to this school, but I hadn't seen her yet. Probably just as well, with everything I'd found out lately.

Mrs. Larson from across the hall reminded me that I would be watching the children at recess. I gathered the children after lunch and took them outside. The sun was too hot to stand under, so I stood off to the side by a tree that provided some shade. I watched over the children as they took turns going down the slide and swinging on the swings.

My mind started to think about Samantha and decided that I'd stop over at Michele's house and see what was going on. I wanted to find out why Michele hadn't transferred Samantha back to Haven Elementary.

I was scanning the playground when my cell phone vibrated in my pants pocket. I slid the phone out and saw an unfamiliar number. Normally, I'd cancel the call when I didn't know the person who was calling, but something inside me told me to answer the phone.

"Hello," I said, feeling my throat tighten.

"Yes, is Mrs. Carla Michaels available?" a woman asked with a southern twang.

"This is she."

"Mrs. Michaels, my name is Eileen Bailey, and I'm calling from the Dakar Correctional Center for Woman in Dakar, Illinois. I'm sorry to be calling ya' like this."

My heart began to pound. Whatever this woman Eileen was calling me about, it didn't sound good.

"I'm afraid there's been an accident with Martha Berkley. There was no one else on the list that had come to see her, but you. So, I figured there must've been some relation between the two of ya'."

Sweat rolled down my back along my spine. I swallowed, moistening my throat. "No, I'm sorry we're..." I stopped myself from telling this woman that we weren't related and figured I'd play along to find out what had happened to Martha.

"What were you about to say?" Eileen questioned."

"Oh, sorry, I'm at work and was talking to someone else. Has something happened to Martha?" I squeezed my eyes shut and shook my head, hoping Eileen couldn't tell I was telling a lie.

"Sorry to bother ya' at work."

"It's no bother. What were you about to tell me?"

"Oh, well, I'm afraid...I'm afraid Martha was killed last night in a fight here at the prison."

I nearly dropped the phone. My mouth fell open, and my throat became dry. I was speechless, shocked even. Martha was dead and now I had no way of getting her DNA.

Chapter 36

I clenched the phone in my hand as I placed it back to my ear. I was literally screwed. I'd never find out the truth—now!

"Mrs. Michaels, I'm so sorry ya' had to find out over the phone. I couldn't find any other means to contact ya'. I…I don't know what to say. Ya' two were close, weren't ya'? Oh, I feel like crap now. It was never in my work ethics to have to tell someone that their relative was killed or had died, for that matter. I'm so sorry for your loss," Eileen said, sounding sympathetic, maybe even on the verge of tears.

I heard every word Eileen said, but the shock was still too new. One of my students called out to me. "Mrs. Michaels, watch how far I can jump," a little girl shouted, twenty, maybe thirty feet in front of where I stood. I smiled a faint smile, waved, and gave a thumbs-up.

"Mrs. Michaels, are ya' all right? Are ya' still on the line?"

"I'm here," I whispered.

"Oh, good! Thought I'd lost ya' there for a minute. Another reason for my call is to ask ya' where you'd like

Martha's remains sent. Is there a particular Funeral home ya' prefer?"

I was taken off-guard when the words slipped off my tongue, "Fuller Funeral Home in Homer Glen, Illinois." *The same funeral home that was used for Tim and Mya's mortuary services.*

"Okay, great! I'll look up the address and let the doctor here know."

"Thanks," I replied.

"Again, I'm so sorry for your loss," Eileen said before the line went dead.

I pushed the phone down into my pocket as a faint bell in the distance *buzzed*. I gathered the children together and headed back inside the school.

$$\sim \ \sim \ \sim \ \sim \ \sim$$

Later that afternoon, I watched as my students climbed onto their buses and were heading home for the day. I sleep-walked through the rest of the day as if nothing had ever happened. No, actually, I didn't want to think about what Eileen had told me—and what was I thinking?— telling that woman to send Martha's remains to the same place my husband's final preparations had been done. Well, I couldn't really blame myself; the call had caught me when I least expected it. I acted without thinking. Something I'd been doing a lot lately.

I made my way back to the classroom and gathered my things. Within ten minutes, I was seated in my car and driving to Fuller Funeral Home to talk to the Funeral Director. I parked by the front door and exited the car.

I grabbed the handle of the large oak door, and nearly lost my balance. The door was locked. I tried the other door, but it was also locked. I glanced around, noticing a doorbell. I pressed the bell and waited as it echoed through the building.

Five, maybe ten minutes had passed; hell, it could've been longer, I wasn't sure, as I waited for someone to open the door. Just as I turned to walk back to my car, I heard the sound of a deadbolt click and stopped in my tracks, turning back to face the door.

One of the doors creaked open, a chill ran through my spine, but I didn't see anyone. I took a step closer, then another one, until I was in front of the open doorway.

"Hello," I called out. My body began to tremble. An old man's face sprung out from behind the door. I let out a scream, stepped back, causing my foot to fall into a small hole in the ground, and landed on my butt.

"Oh, my, let me help you, Miss," the scraggily old man said, reaching out his long wispy fingers. "I didn't mean to scare you. I keep forgetting that I need to stand in the opening after I open the door. I can't say you're the first one I've scared doing that."

I slid my hand in his, being careful not to pull him down. Once I was back on my feet, I dusted off my butt. I took a step and winced, as pain shot through my foot.

"Oh, my, you're hurt, aren't you, Miss?" he asked.

"I think I twisted my ankle," I replied.

"Oh, no. Come in and I'll get you some ice to put on that hurt foot of yours."

I wasn't sure if I should just go home or take him up on his offer and go inside. I looked at his sad old face and decided to let him help me, since he was the one who'd scared me and made me fall to the ground.

I took ahold of his arm and hobbled inside. Lucky for me, the office sat around the corner of the entrance. He helped me to a leather sofa by the wall, and then scurried out the door.

He returned minutes later with a bag of frozen peas. "This works better than ice cubes in a towel," he replied. "My wife, Gilda, God rest her soul, always used a bag of frozen peas from the store. Sometimes, she even used a bag of frozen corn. Either works just as well."

"Thanks," I whispered.

Silence filled the air between us. *Should I say something to him?* I thought. No, I'd wait for him to talk first, which didn't take long after I'd made the decision.

"So, was there a reason for your visit? I'm assuming someone close to you has died." The old man stated, knowingly.

"Well," I hesitated. "We weren't actually close. To be honest with you, I don't really even know her. I knew of her. Her daughter was in my class at Haven Elementary."

"Oh," the old man replied. He blinked several times before speaking. "I'm not sure I fully understand."

I explained with little detail about Martha and the phone call I received earlier.

"So, you're having Martha Berkley brought to this funeral home, but you aren't a relative?"

"I guess if you want to put it that way, no, I'm not related to her, nor do I intend to pay for her funeral," I stated, firmly.

"Then who will pay for this? We don't normally have free caskets, you know. Funerals aren't free. They can cost thousands, unless you have them cremated."

"Cremated?" I questioned.

"Yes, you do know what that is, don't you?"

"Well, yes, of course, I do," I nodded. "What will happen to her if no one pays for her burial? Where would she go?"

"Go? Well, if there's no family, and no Last Will and Testament, then the government contractor will take care of the funeral," the old man paused. "Why would you agree to this on the phone if you're not even a relative?"

"I was caught off-guard when the woman told me. I guess I was in a state of shock, you might say. The woman had said I was the only one to come see Martha so she automatically assumed we were related. I was actually going down to see her on Saturday, but I got the call that she was killed," I rambled on. "What do I do now?"

"Once the remains arrive, I will call the county and let them know what's going on."

"Oh, okay. Thank you. I'm so sorry for the misunderstanding. I suppose I've had a lot going on lately and wasn't thinking clearly."

I almost forgot why I needed to see Martha. I still needed her DNA, but that wasn't going to happen now that she was dead, or could I ask this nice old man to give me a sample of Martha's blood, if she still had blood. I didn't know what happened to the inside of a body once the person was dead. Surely, the organs just like the heart stopped working. I wasn't sure, but could I ask this kind man? Would he do that for me? I couldn't just come right out and say I needed Martha's DNA to prove if she were the mother of my husband's daughter, or possibly his sister, could I? Would he think I was insane? Did I really even care? I needed to find out.

"Are you feeling all right, Miss?" The old man asked.

"What? Yes, I'm fine. Sometimes I get to thinking and kind of zone out for a while. At least that's what I've been told."

"Yeah, I do that sometimes myself. My son keeps telling me he'll put me in one of those nursing homes if I don't stop. I told him I'd rather be dead than to be put in one of those places," the old man laughed. "Guess I shouldn't say that at a funeral home, huh?" the old man laughed. "I think my Bradley is about the same age as you. He hasn't been married you know," he added.

Was this man being serious? Was he trying to set us up on a date or something? I smiled. I didn't know what to think about this kind man. I knew I should just ask him about what was rolling around in my head so I can get out of here. I took in a deep breath, the words rolling down my tongue as I opened my mouth, "I hate…" I was interrupted.

"Dad, are you in here?" Bradley said as he entered the room. He stopped, looked at me. "Mrs. Michaels, is there something I can help you with?" Bradley smiled, and then added, "I hope my father hasn't bored you with his stories?"

"No, it's fine," I replied. The bag of cold peas hit the floor as I slid my legs off the sofa.

"What's with the bag of peas?" Bradley said. "Dad, did you forget to show your face again when you opened the door? How many times have I told you, not to stand behind the door after you open it?"

I stood, wincing slightly from the pain in my ankle. Bradley hadn't seemed to notice. "No, it was my fault. I tripped and twisted my ankle. Your dad isn't at fault—really."

"Oh, well, are you okay? Do you need to go to the hospital?"

"What? No, I'll be fine. Just need to walk it off." I looked over at the old man, smiled and winked at him before his son noticed.

"All right then. Is there something I can help you with? I'm assuming you're here for a reason?" Bradley questioned.

"Oh, yes, I almost forgot why I came here, though your father has been a great help. There is a person by the name of Martha Berkley being transported to your Mortuary in the next day or two. I was informing your father here that I'm not related to the woman and will not be paying for the cremation." I told Bradley the same story I'd told the old man. "So, I'll be going now. Thanks for the frozen vegetables." I grabbed my purse from the floor, walked out the door, and to my car.

Chapter 37

Before heading home, I decided to stop at Michele's house and pay her a visit. I knocked several times before the same little boy I had seen last time answered the door.

"Hi, is Michele home?"

"No, she's at the hospital," the little boy replied.

"Oh, is everything okay?" I asked, concerned.

"I guess so," the boy shrugged his shoulders.

I questioned, "You're not here alone are you?" I pried my head to get a look inside.

"No, my neighbor is here."

"Well, that's good. Don't want you at home all by yourself," I stated.

"I'm not alone. The other kids that live here are all upstairs playing games."

"Is one of those kids Samantha Berkley?" I remembered from the time before that there was two Samantha's living in the house.

"No, she's the reason why Michele had to go to the hospital."

"What happened?" My heart raced hard beneath my chest. "Is she okay?" Of course, she wasn't okay. Why else would she have to go to the hospital?

"I think she fell down the stairs. I didn't see it happen, but I heard Michele screaming so I came out of my room and saw Samantha lying at the bottom of the stairs."

"Oh, dear God! You wouldn't happen to know if they went to Silver Cross Hospital, do you?"

The boy shook his head.

"Can I talk to your neighbor? Maybe she knows which one they went to."

The boy turned and ran quickly up the stairs. A minute later, a middle-aged woman came trotting down the stairs and into the front room. She wore a smile on her face, big like a clown and seemed happier than horseshit on a hot summer's day.

"Well, hello. How can I help you?" the woman sang, smiling her full set of teeth.

I introduced myself and repeated what the boy had said. "Would you happen to know which hospital she was taken to?"

"The ambulance came and took her to Silver Cross. Do you know where that's at?" the woman asked.

Unfortunately, I did know the hospital all too well. "Yes, thank you," I replied as I turned and ran down the stairs to my car without saying another word, and forgetting all about my twisted and hurt ankle.

In record time, I drove to the hospital, parked the car, and ran to the entrance. I had no clue where I needed to go and marched straight to the receptionist desk. I explained my circumstances to the elder woman behind the desk and was instructed to head to the emergency department on the south end of the building.

I had to tell myself several times to calm the hell down and take deep breaths. No good would come out of this if they were to throw me out of the hospital for my hysterical behavior.

I turned the corner and saw a nurse's station along the far wall. I quickened my pace, stopping when I reached the desk. Several nurses, holding charts, stood behind the counter.

I cleared my throat, "Excuse me, I'm looking for a Samantha Berkley. Is she here?"

"Yes, she's getting a CT scan. Should be back in a few minutes or so. Are you the parent?" a skinny dark-haired nurse asked.

I shook my head, "Just a friend," I whispered.

"Wait over there," the dark haired nurse pointed to the lobby across the hall. "I'll go get the patient's guardian."

I nodded, turned, and walked to an empty chair near the front row. I placed my purse in my lap, fidgeting with the straps. As often as I'd been to the hospital, I never was the one waiting; I was always the patient.

I drew in a breath, blew it out, repeating this several times. Even with the people talking among themselves, I could hear the ticking of the clock on the wall. I closed my eyes.

Tick. Tick. Tick.

The rhythmic sound played in my head.

"Carla?" a female voice questioned. "What are you doing here?"

My head snapped up and I opened my eyes, Michele was standing just outside the doorway of the lobby. "I went to your house and the little boy Robby told me that Samantha was hurt, and that you'd brought her here."

Michele nodded, "Come with me," she said.

I stood, walked out the door, and followed Michele outside. Michele chose a bench to the right of us and sat down.

"How is she doing?" I asked.

"She's unconscious right now. Well, at least she was when they took her to get a CT scan or X-Ray, whatever machine they use to check people's head injuries."

"What happened?"

"I'm not sure. I was in the kitchen preparing dinner when I heard a scream, and then someone or something was tumbling down the stairs. I dropped what I was doing and ran to see what it was."

"Do you know what could have caused her to fall?"

Michele bowed her head before continuing, "Samantha's been having problems with the other Samantha."

"What kind of problems?"

"Bullying, name calling, that sort of thing. Samantha Cripps didn't come from an abusive home like Samantha Berkley. Samantha's parents were killed in a car accident, two years ago. She has no living relatives. She's been in and out of foster homes ever since."

I shook my head, "Poor girl. Why do you think she's been bullying Samantha?"

"Ever since Tim had come to see her and now you, she's…well, I believe she envies her. She has no one. No one comes to visit with her. Samantha Berkley has been nothing but nice to her, but no matter what she does or says, Samantha Cripps replies with hateful words and hateful actions."

"So, you think she has something to do with Samantha falling down the stairs?" I questioned.

"I know she does."

"What makes you say that?"

"She was standing at the top of the stairs with a huge smile on her face."

"Oh, my God! That's awful!"

"I've already called the coordinator at social services, and he's having her removed first thing tomorrow morning."

"What will happen to her?" I asked.

"Since she's showing signs of physical abuse, they'll have her evaluated before being placed at another home. She might have some mental issues, things I'm not qualified to help her with."

I nodded.

Minutes slipped by, the absence of sound filled the air between us. A nurse from the ER came outside, calling for Michele. We both stood at the same time, as the nurse waved us inside. I followed closely behind Michele. The nurse pulled back a set of curtains, revealing Samantha lying on a bed with her eyes closed.

"I'll go get the doctor. You both wait here."

We both nodded simultaneously as we made our way to each side of the bed. I reached out and took Samantha's hand in mine, using my free hand to brush the hair away on her forehead, being careful of the white gauze wrapped around her head.

The chain links rattled as the curtain was moved aside and a tall Hispanic man in a white doctor's coat walked in, carrying a clipboard. He stopped, looked up, then back down at the chart in his hand.

"Michele Channels, I presume?" the doctor said, looking at me.

"No, I'm Carla Michaels. She's Michele Channels," I nudged my head towards Michele on the other side of the bed.

His eyes moved, "Michele, you're the guardian of Samantha Berkley, is that correct?"

"Yes, that's right."

He searched through the papers, "Due to her head trauma, she's lost consciousness and there's some swelling around her brain, but nothing that seems life threating. We should see an improvement within a couple of days. In addition to the skull fracture, she's lost a significant amount of blood as well. The bleeding has stopped, but she's going to need a blood transfusion."

"Blood transfusion?" I questioned.

"Yes, Samantha has a rare blood type," Dr. Sage glanced down at his notes, "AB negative, to be exact. What we did have in our blood bank wasn't enough; she'll still need another three pints, if not more."

My mind flashed back to the DNA results. If I had read the report correctly, Martha was A+ and John Berkley an O+. I wasn't sure what Tim was; I never needed to know his blood type. I, on the other hand, knew mine well. "I'm AB negative," I whispered. "I can give her my blood."

"We'll need to take a sample of your blood first, and then mix it with a sample of Samantha's to make sure that no problems occur, but in any case that shouldn't take too much time."

I smiled and looked over at Michele. Michele nodded in return, indicating for me to go now. I followed the doctor out of the enclosure and towards the nurse's station where he informed a short brunette woman, who didn't look much older than twenty-one, to place Samantha Berkley in a private room for two. Then, Dr. Sage informed a different nurse to accompany me to the lab where I'd give them a sample of my blood to be checked.

"I want you to inform the lab that this is an emergency. Once the blood is checked, she will need to be brought to Samantha Berkley's room for the blood transfusion," Dr. Sage ordered. The nurse nodded and quickly led me down the hall.

Thirty minutes later, I was ushered to the fifth floor and was handed a gown. I changed in the bathroom of Samantha's room and slipped under the thick white sheets.

A different nurse entered the room, pushing in a cart. The nurse swabbed my left arm and inserted the needle. In an instant, my blood ran through the tube to a bag and then into Samantha's arm.

After about fifteen minutes, my eyes started to get heavy. I was tired and weak. I hadn't even had time for dinner, more less something to drink. My eyes closed without thought.

Chapter
38

When I came to an hour later, I noticed a Band-Aid on my left arm and an IV on my right. Dr. Sage, who had just left our room, said I was dehydrated and my immune system was low; that's why I had passed out.

I turned my head and looked over at Samantha who still seemed to be unresponsive. The doctor said it would take some time before the swelling would go down, but... but there was still a chance Samantha might not remember things. We all had to wait and see when and if she woke up.

I wasn't aware someone had entered the room until I heard a voice.

"How are you feeling?" asked Michele as she made her way to the foot of the bed.

"I'm fine," I replied. "How long was I out?"

"Couple hours."

I nodded.

"Have you been here the whole time?"

"Yeah, pretty much. I stepped out to call my neighbor and let her know what was going on, and that I'll be home soon. I just wanted to come back to the room and see how you were doing."

"Oh, that's awfully nice of you," I said.

Had I been wrong about Michele? Just because I'd read in Tim's journals about their conversation didn't mean she was a bad person, right? She'd been nothing but nice to me. Maybe it was me who was the one acting snobbish, not Michele. Sure, that was definitely a possibility; my husband and daughter had just died. I'd read his journals, and then found more of them hidden away in his office. All the secrets and lies he'd been hiding away, for what? A rainy day? Had he ever planned to tell me the truth? I'd never know, would I? Then, it was a good thing that I'd found his books. "His secret life", I'd called it.

"Carla, are you all right? You feeling okay?"

"What?" I asked, jerking my head up and towards Michele's voice.

"I was talking to you, but you looked like you were in another world. Do you want me to get the doctor?"

"No!" I nearly shouted. "Sorry, I'm fine, really. I was just thinking about something that had happened long ago," I gave a slight smile. *It wasn't that long ago*, the voice in my head reminded me.

"So, Dr. Sage wants you to stay for the night?" Michele questioned.

"Yes, just for the night. Before you came into the room, he said he wanted to admit me for observation because I was so weak from not eating well. If it were up to me, I wouldn't step foot inside another hospital if my life depended on it."

"I hear, ya'. I'm not a big fan of doctors myself."

Silence crept in between us, neither one looking at the other. I began to feel uncomfortable. An uneasy feeling flowed through my body. Just for that split second, that mere instant, I thought I felt Tim's presence around me.

Was it the fact I'd been reading his journals that made me think of him? On the other hand, was it Michele? They'd been working together for years, or was it longer than I thought? Maybe it was time I asked this woman in front of me some questions I've been *wanting*, no, *needing* to know. Could it be possible, Michele knew Tim better than I thought I knew him? That to me wasn't even a question, but more of a fact; an actual truth that chipped away pieces of my heart.

I hadn't really known my husband as well as I thought I had. Does anyone really know their own spouse better than their parents, siblings, or friends? In all honesty, how well do we know our own family? I wouldn't know that either; I was an only child with no parents, no siblings. I guess no one really knew everything about the one they love. At least that's what it seemed like to me.

"Do you need anything before I go?" Michele asked.

"What?" I answered, shaking the scattered thoughts from my mind.

"I asked if you needed anything before I go?"

I wanted answers, but was it the right time to ask them? Did I care if it weren't? I'd been kept in the dark for years; hell, since I'd met Tim! "Do you have a minute? I'd like to ask you some personal questions. Questions about Tim that I hope you can clarify for me."

Michele's eyes widened, slightly, before looking away from me. "I'll try to answer what I can," Michele replied, swallowing.

I pointed to the empty spot near the foot of the bed. "Please, sit," I requested. "Did you know Tim was adopted?"

"Yes, I was his foster parent until the Michaels's adopted him."

I nodded, "And you've kept close with him throughout the years, I presume?"

"I guess you can say we have. I was in my early twenties when I became a foster parent; shortly after that, Tim was brought to me. Even after he was adopted we kept in contact, then after he graduated from college and he came back to Illinois, we started working together, helping children find good homes."

"What do you know about the Berkley's? Did you know Tim requested a DNA test to be done on them before the hearing?" I swallowed, "before he died?"

"What?" Michele shook her head. "Why would he do a DNA test on them? Unless he found out something that he hasn't shared with any of us. Something he hadn't gotten a chance to tell us."

"The results came back the day that he died, but they were inconclusive."

"What does that mean?" Michele leaned forward as if we were whispering secrets to one another.

"John Berkley is not, was not, Samantha's biological father. Martha's DNA doesn't show that she is the mother, but it also doesn't exclude her. The other day I received the results back that Tim and Martha could be Samantha's parents, but..." I wasn't sure if I was ready to confront the truth, but I knew I had to. Maybe telling Michele would bring me closer to knowing what Tim had kept from me.

"But…" I paused again, "the woman I talked to on the phone, Barbara Collins, said that they could somehow be related, possibly brother and sister, but she wasn't certain and didn't want to say they were definitely related. It didn't mean they were Samantha's parents, either, but it was still possible. As far as I know, Tim doesn't have any siblings. I did find where he'd written down Martha's mothers name being Blackstine. It's either that, or he was cheating on me and got her pregnant with Samantha," I stated.

Michele's head jolted up. "No! Tim would never cheat on you! He'd never have an affair. You said Martha's mother's name was Blackstine?"

"Yes, Lisa Blackstine."

"There's got to be some mistake. Tim's biological mother's name was Lisa Blackstone, not Blackstine," Michele stated.

"Oh," I replied. "That definitely could've been a mistake on his part or the newspapers. He was killed before he was able to find the truth. Although, the names were so close that anyone could've made that mistake," I concluded.

"Yes, you're right," Michele agreed.

"Well, here's another tricky part. I need Martha's DNA along with mine to find out the results."

"Why do you need to have yours checked?"

"Barbara suggested that I have mine checked along with Martha's, Tim's, and Samantha's."

"But that doesn't make sense?"

"How so?" I asked.

"Martha being Tim's sister? It just doesn't add up," Michele stated. "There was never any mention of Tim having a sister."

I didn't want to think about that now. I needed to figure out how to get Martha's DNA before it was too late. "Martha was killed in prison, and I don't know how to get a sample of her blood or saliva for the test."

"That's easy. I can put in a call and have them set me up with some of her blood and hair, if you want."

"Really? You can do that?" I said.

"Sure, I'll just need to know where Martha Berkley's body was taken to."

I filled Michele in on the call I received and where the body was sent. Why hadn't I gone to Michele about this earlier? That was a stupid thought. I already knew the answer to that.

Chapter 39

Early the next morning, I was released from the hospital. I pulled into my driveway and climbed out of the car. Before I was able to walk up the stoned path to my front door, Deanna from across the street was calling my name.

"Carla, wait up," Deanna called out as she jogged across the street. "Is everything okay? I didn't see you come home last night," Deanna said as she stood beside me, slightly out of breath.

I wasn't about to announce to my neighbor about giving blood to a student of mine that was lying unconscious in the hospital with a head trauma. Although I had shared secrets with her the other day, I'd wait for a non-hectic day to reveal the rest of what I had just found out. "Yeah, I got to talking to an old friend and decided to stay overnight." *Well, it was somewhat the truth*, I thought.

"Oh, okay. Well, anyway, I was talking to Brice and once you have the samples, he'll do the test for you," she smiled.

It had slipped my mind about Brice doing the test. "Great, I should have everything in a couple of days. Should I bring them over when I have them?"

"Yes, or I can send Brice over to retrieve them. That way if you have any questions he can answer them for you. He said it'd only take a day, maybe two, to get the results of the test."

I'd know within a couple of days all the secrets Tim had hid from me, but mostly, who Samantha's parents were. I smiled, "Well, I have some things I need to take care of."

"Oh, sure, that's no problem. Just let me know if you need anything. Besides, I need to get back to writing. I've been slacking these past couple of weeks. You know with the weather and all. Sometimes the absence of the sun will make you depressed, you know," Deanna stated as a fact.

The truth was, I knew all too well what depression was. However, I didn't think the sun had too much to do with it, but now that Deanna had mentioned it, it did make more sense. The cold bitter season, with no sun for days, weeks, sometimes a month or two, it was depressing. Although I had missed a month by staying in bed, the weather hadn't been all that bad lately, with warms days and cool evenings. It was actually quite nice.

I tossed the thought aside not wanting to get it into my head at this very moment in time. "Thanks for letting me know about the test." I took a step towards the house, making it obvious that I was done talking.

Deanna must have sensed me pulling away and spoke, "I'll see you soon. I know you have to get to work," Deanna said as she waved goodbye.

"Okay, see ya'," I sang, sounding more cheerful than I meant to sound, but then realizing I did have to get ready for work. Glancing down at my wristwatch, I was thankful I had an hour to get ready before I had to leave again.

Once inside my home, I tossed my purse on the bench next to the door and went into the kitchen. While Michele was off getting the DNA sample that I needed to confirm who the parents were, I was going to finish reading the rest of Tim's journal, but unfortunately, it would have to wait until I got home from work, or I could take the journal with me. Yes, that was a thought too.

After setting up the coffeemaker, I went upstairs to get ready. By the time I came back down, the coffee was finished, and I poured myself a cup. I grabbed the book off the table and reclined in the chair on the back porch. I'd just read a couple of pages, and then head off to work.

September 23rd, 2007

> *Carla made it through surgery and is walking around. The doctor told me in private that he removed five of her eggs and that he'll keep them sealed in the freezer until I'm ready for them.*
>
> *I've already been talking with a woman who will be our surrogate mother.*

"What the hell?" I mumbled aloud. My mind was spinning out of control. I couldn't believe what I was reading. A surrogate mother? To carry our baby? Was he nuts? What would make him want to do something like that? And, if he did, where's our baby? I needed to continue reading to find out the answers to all my questions.

I'm not sure about telling Carla just yet; I'd like to make sure the baby makes it to full-term. She has had too much to deal with and another death of a baby would crush the life she has left inside her.

I plan to keep a log on the growth of our baby, so one day she can read it, and know what the surrogate mother went through. I pray this works and I can give Carla the baby she deserves.

My mouth dropped open; I was beyond shocked. At least for a moment, until everything started to make sense to me and fell into place like a puzzle. I knew without a doubt that the DNA test would prove what happened eight years ago. I needed to finish reading the journal, but knew that it would have to wait until later. I drank down the rest of my coffee and left for work.

Chapter 40

The morning rushed by, and lunch quickly arrived. The children were having their lunch and then would be going outside for recess with Mrs. Larson today.

I sat behind my desk and opened the book to the page I'd left off at.

September 25th, 2007

I'm sitting in my office in downtown Chicago, waiting as patiently as I can for my one-hour lunchtime to arrive.

I'm nervous to meet the woman who might be the surrogate mother to Carla and my baby. I want so much for this to work out, for her to be the one. I told her to meet me at Millennium Park at twelve-thirty <u>sharp!</u> I'm praying this all works out, and we finally have a baby.

* * *

September 25th, 2007

She's agreed to be a surrogate mother for me, but I told her there needs to be some medical procedures done before we begin. Blood work to check that she has no diseases or cancer, nothing that'll harm the fetus. I gave her the appointment card and told her once the tests come back and everything looks great, we will meet with the doctor and start the process. This woman agreed on the payment for going through with this. I told her that I'd pay her $2,000 dollars a month plus all medical bills and procedures, and then we'll go our separate ways after the baby is born.

* * *

October 6th, 2007

The doctor phoned me that the results looked good. She's a healthy twenty-four-year old white female with no medical history or medical concerns. I set up an appointment for

*us to meet and have them inject her
with Carla's eggs and my sperm.*

I was beside myself; I couldn't believe what I was reading. *Tim had actually found this woman and impregnated her. What was he thinking? Had he lost faith in me getting pregnant? This was eight years ago, after I'd already lost two babies,* I noted.

After thinking about it for a few seconds, I couldn't honestly blame him for doing it, but he should've confided in me. Tim shouldn't have gone out on his own and picked a complete stranger and trust her with our baby. I had to read more to find out what happened because in all reality we hadn't raised a baby, so something must have happened.

October 9th, 2007

We met with the doctor today, but I didn't stay in the room while he performed the procedure. It didn't take as long as I thought it would.

The doctor said it would take a few weeks to see if the egg takes and is fertilized. If it doesn't work, there was still a chance to try again.

Part of me is excited, yet nervous all at the same time. Carla and I could be parents. I don't want to get overly excited, mostly because of what happened to Carla after losing two babies. I've decided to wait the full-

term of the pregnancy to tell her. No sense getting Carla's hopes up and then dropping a bomb on her.

* * *

October 31st, 2007

We just left the doctor's office and she's pregnant. I should feel ecstatic, but part of me feels sad that I can't share it with Carla. She'll be so excited to have a baby.

* * *

November 27th, 2007

She's four weeks into the pregnancy and all is well so far. Still not getting my hopes up, it's best to wait this out.

I read a few more pages before my lunchtime ended and the students returned to class. I'd have to wait until later to finish the journal. Right now, I had to clear my mind and teach my class, but was feeling thankful tomorrow was Friday.

Chapter 41

I was exhausted by the time I'd pulled into my driveway and parked the car. As I was getting ready to open the door, I saw Deanna from across the street. She was stepping off her porch and heading towards the driveway.

Was she coming over to see me? I questioned. I didn't know if I should open the door or wait to see what Deanna was going to do. It wasn't like I was trying to avoid her, was I? Yeah, probably, but that was only because I wanted to finish reading the rest of Tim's journal and find out what had happened to our baby, and whether or not Samantha was ours.

I glanced at the side-mirror and saw that Deanna had retrieved her mail and was now heading back inside her house. I let out a breath and waited until I didn't see my neighbor any longer. A minute later, I opened the car door and headed inside.

Once in the kitchen, I poured myself a glass of ice tea and headed to the porch out back with Tim's journal in hand. I sat comfortably in the chair and opened the book to the page where I'd left off.

March 30th, 2008

She's now six months along, and everything seems to be going good. I've been meeting with her at the doctor's office and the baby looks healthy in the sonogram. We found out today that it's a GIRL!

I'm so excited! Carla will be so pleased. She's always wanted a baby girl. I, on the other hand, just wanted a healthy baby.

Three more months to go, and then I can tell her all about it, though I'll have to, since I'll be bringing the baby home with me.

* * *

May 14th, 2008

I can't believe it! This woman is trying to blackmail me! I've been giving her money every month and now she wants more!

She said if I don't continue to pay her, then she'll keep the baby. I knew I should've had her sign a paper before going through with the procedure. Payments are supposed to stop when the baby is born. That was our agreement, but now she's getting possessive, saying I'll never see the child ever again.

I can't continue to pay her; Carla will find out eventually, and I can't have that—she can't know I had paid someone to have our child...

I stopped reading; a single tear ran down my cheek. This woman took our baby and ran. She hid her from us because Tim refused to pay her more money. I didn't blame him really. No, I understood, but what bothered me the most was the fact that he'd kept this enormous secret from me all these years. We could've fought for the baby, but I'd never even known about her. Our only child.

My thoughts shifted, and now I thought of Samantha. She could be my daughter. I knew, for this to be all done, what I needed to do.

I fanned the remaining pages of the journal and saw that there weren't many pages to go. I'd finish reading the book before I did anything.

June 21st, 2008

She went into labor at six thirty-seven this morning; She had a baby girl.

I told her that I'd give her ten thousand dollars—no more! At first she agreed, but later when I came back with the cash, she'd changed her mind, said she wanted more.

Standing in the room was a burly man, who looked like he lifted weights every day. The man, not sure of his name, said I could have the baby for five hundred thousand dollars. When I told him that I didn't have that kind of cash, he replied, "Then we keep the baby!" He smacked his fist into his other palm. The sound made a deathly smack as I envisioned his palm being my face.

I gave Carla and me a baby; yet again, I had lost her at the same time...

Tears flowed down my face, my mascara leaving black lines as I cried. I wept not only for the loss I didn't know I'd had, but also for the pain that Tim had endured. For years, he'd kept this to himself, not telling a soul. At least no one I was aware of.

I finished the remaining pages and closed the book. I looked up and out at the backyard. For the first time, I actually felt okay. Not happy, nor sad, just plain old-content.

Chapter 42

I walked back inside just as the doorbell rang. I placed my glass on the table along with Tim's journal and made my way to the door.

Michele stood in front of me, holding an envelope. "Hi, Carla. May I come in?" she asked.

Without saying a word, I moved aside. Michele quickly walked in, heading straight to the kitchen and sat down.

"Michele, is everything okay? Is Samantha all right?" I asked, feeling nervous and scared all at the same time.

I shut the door and followed her into the kitchen, sitting down across from her. "Talk to me. What's going on?"

Without saying a word, Michele slid an envelope across the table.

"You want me to open this?" I asked.

She nodded.

I picked up the envelope, pushed the metal prongs together and slipped my hand inside, pulling out several pieces of paper. I looked at Michele before reading the letter out loud.

Dear Mrs. Michaels,

I'm writing to inform you that you are Samantha Marie Berkley's biological mother. I was contacted after the sudden death of your husband Tim Michaels by his attorney Robert Beckon.

Robert Beckon has filed the papers for the release of Samantha Marie Berkley to your care as of April 25th, 2015. The papers enclosed are the child's birth certificate and medical records.

I'm so sorry for your loss. Tim was a great man, a great attorney, and a great friend. It is in my deepest regret to have to share with you his illness.

My breath hitched in my throat. Illness? What illness? Tim didn't… Tim hadn't told me of an illness. He hadn't… I hadn't known anything was wrong. My mind whirled around inside my head as I looked over at Michele. I felt almost dizzy, light-headed, all of a sudden. I looked back down at the paper, I needed to finish reading it, and find out what else I never knew about my own husband.

Four months ago, right before his sudden death, Tim had confided in me that he had an aneurysm in his brain. When I asked the coroner about a cause of death, he concluded, which is also enclosed, that the initial shock of the bullet entering his chest most likely caused the blood vessel to rupture in his brain, which then instantly killed him.

Again, I'm so sorry for your loss, as I wish there was something I or someone else could've done to save his life in the end.

If you have any further questions pertaining to these documents, and, or need more information, please feel free to give me a call direct at the number provided below.

Sincerely,
Judge Henry Cole
555-111-3344

I wiped the tears away, trying to get ahold of myself, but as the words registered in my brain, I crumbled to the floor.

Chapter 43

I hadn't slept a wink last night as I cried continuously over the death of my husband. To me it was new, as if it had just happened. Tim knew he was going to die, and that's why he started preparing himself, getting all the journals together and writing these letters to me. He wanted to make sure I knew about everything if he died, when he died. Although, he was working on the DNA tests and finding out if Samantha was ours, what would he have done if she were? Would he have fought to have it proven that we were, in fact, her biological parents? Or, was he thinking of adopting her after the judge sentenced Martha and her husband to prison?

These were all questions I had to file away, never to be answered. Because in all honesty, Tim was the only one who could answer them, and he was no longer here. Now that I know the truth about what he did, I would need to be the strong one and raise the daughter he gave us. The daughter I had always wanted.

Before Michele had left last night, she handed me one more item. It was the DNA samples of Martha Berkley. I had questioned myself if I even needed to do anything with the DNA. The letter had stated I was Samantha's biological mother. Therefore, why would I need to do the test? Tim had also written that Martha was the surrogate mother.

No, wait! He'd never said her name in the book. He referred to the woman as a she or her. I had assumed it was Martha, but that was what didn't make sense. If it were Martha, and he'd known this when he started the case, then why would he need to do a DNA test to show that she, Martha, was not Samantha's real mother? Tim had already known she wasn't so what was he really doing a DNA test for? Was it to see if she was his sister? That was definitely possible. I would contact Brice and have him run all of our DNA and be done with it once and for all.

I glanced at the clock to see how much time I had before I needed to be at the school. It was Friday, and even though I had just gone back to work on Monday, I wanted the week to be over and finally just decided to call in sick. I needed to finish the DNA tests and bring Samantha home, those were the two most important things to me.

I gathered everything I needed to give Brice and walked out the door. There was a slight breeze in the air and the smell of lilacs enticed my senses. I loved the smell of spring, but mostly seeing all my flowers blooming and coming to life after the long winter.

I stopped at the end of my driveway, looked both ways, and made my way to my neighbor's front door. Deanna's son Brent answered the door and allowed me to come inside.

I stood in the foyer, while Brent went and retrieved Brice.

"Carla, it's so nice to see you again. Won't you please step into my office and we'll talk," Brice said with his French accent as he motioned me to follow him.

I nodded and quickened my pace behind him as he disappeared behind a wall. Seconds later, I entered, closed the door, and took the chair in front of his desk.

"Please, excuse the mess I have here," Brice stated.

"Don't worry about it, I know you're a busy man," I replied.

"That I am. So, what do you have for me?"

"I assume Deanna has filled you in on what has been going on?" I said, and then continued after he nodded. "I have recently come into some findings so I guess what I'm looking for now is to see who this Martha woman is. Who she's related to, and what kind of relationship they had. Does that make sense?"

"Yes, I understand. Is there anything else I need to know before I start the testing?"

I filled him in on what Tim's journals said and the letter with the birth certificate, and that I was the biological mother of the child.

Brice wrote all this down and clipped it to the file I had given him. "I should know in the next two, maybe three, days," Brice said.

"Great, I'll be waiting patiently. Right now, I need to get to the hospital and see how my daughter is doing," I replied. The words sounded foreign coming from my throat. I have a daughter. A seven-year-old daughter; I honestly couldn't believe it myself. "Brice," I cleared my throat, "Could you do one more thing for me?"

He nodded.

"Could you please do a DNA test on Samantha and me, you know just to make sure? I guess I just need proof that this is real. That she is, without a doubt, my daughter."

"Trust me, Carla, I'll double check everything before I give you the results. I don't want you to have to worry about anything. We'll get to the bottom of this so you can move on with your life."

"Thanks so much, Brice. Say hello to Deanna for me," I said as I gripped the arm of the chair and stood.

"I'll do that. I'll talk to you soon." Brice stood and walked me out.

~ ~ ~ ~ ~

I arrived at the hospital fifteen minutes later. A shiver ran down my spine the minute I entered the building. Had it been because I'd lost my babies here? Or, was something wrong? No! I wouldn't allow myself to believe something bad had happened to Samantha.

I quickened my step and pressed the up button near the elevator. The elevator *dinged* and the doors slid open. I had to wait until all of the people climbed out before I could get inside. "Come on people, move, will ya?" I mumbled under my breath.

I hit floor number five and stood glued to the entrance, waiting to get off and see Samantha. The elevator came to a sudden stop; the doors opened and I quickly stepped out, looking for the numbers on the wall to show me where I needed to go.

I hadn't paid any attention when I was here the day before, what room Samantha was in. I stopped at the nurse's station and asked.

"Room #513," the woman replied. "Turn left at the end of the hall; it'll be on the right."

I nodded, stepped away from the desk, and quickly made my way down the hall. When I finally arrived at the room, the door was slightly ajar. I reached out and pushed the door open, stepping forward. Once inside the room, I saw Samantha sitting up in her bed.

The anxiety I had disappeared when she turned her head and saw me standing in the doorway. "Mrs. Michaels, you came to see me," Samantha sang with a smile on her face.

I smiled back at her and hurried to the side of the bed. "You're awake?"

"Yeah, I woke up sometime last night. My head still hurts a little, but the nurse gave me something to take the pain away. It don't hurt that much now," Samantha replied.

"Well, that's good news. Speaking of good news," I smiled again. "I have something I'd like to share with you."

"Really, I love surprises."

"Me too," I replied. "I received some papers yesterday. They say that you can come live with me. What do you think about that?" I asked.

I held my breath waiting for her to say something, anything. For some reason I was nervous. Would Samantha want to come live with me? Would she like the fact that I was her mother? Yes, of course she'd love the idea. Samantha talked highly of me. I'd heard it in the recording.

"Really? I can come live with you?" Samantha shrieked in excitement! She reached out and hugged me around my waist.

I was her mother? How would I tell her? What would she think? I didn't want to confuse her about the other people who had raised her for seven years. Well, in all honesty, they raised her, but also abused her. Parents aren't supposed to abuse their child. I wasn't sure if Samantha would understand, but I really wanted to tell her; yet I decided I'd wait until the results came back and proved without a reasonable doubt that we were mother and daughter! I wrapped my arms around my daughter as I stood next to her bed.

"Yay! I'm so happy I'm going to be living with you. I wish Mr. Michaels was here too, but you said he's in heaven watching over us. Does that mean he can't come and visit once in a while?"

"Well," I thought for a moment. "He can't actually come and visit because he's already here with us," I pointed to my heart and then to Samantha's. "He'll always be with us, no matter where we are.

Chapter 44

I had gone to Michele's and collected all of Samantha's things while she remained in the hospital. I also made a trip to the mall and bought her some new clothes and things I thought she'd like in her new room. I'd wait and take her shopping for a new bedroom set, when she recovered.

I had decided to take the baby crib to Goodwill, but Deanna had seen me trying to get the crib in the backseat of my car, which was a really stupid thing to do, considering I had a car. She came over and asked if she could have it, as she excitedly told me they were expecting.

Two days later on Sunday morning, Samantha was released from the hospital and into my care. We were sitting on the swing on the back porch when the doorbell rang. "I'll be right back," I said as I slipped off the seat and headed inside to the front door.

"Hey, Carla," Brice greeted when I opened the door.

My throat closed as I tried to swallow. I knew what he was here for, what he had in his hand. "Hi, come in, please," I replied as I motioned for him to enter.

We proceeded to the family room, away from earshot. I wanted to know before Samantha overheard, especially if it were bad news.

"Well," I swallowed, my body beginning to shake.

"Open it," Brice smiled as he handed over the envelope. "You might want to sit before you read what it says," he suggested.

"Is it bad? Does it say she isn't my daughter?" I blurted out. I watched Brice for a reaction, but didn't see one. I took the envelope and sat down.

After a couple of breaths, in through my nose and out my mouth, I opened the flap and pulled the papers out. The first one had a bunch of numbers on it, which confused me. I didn't know how to read one of these.

"Brice, just tell me what it means!" I said a little too loud.

Brice took the papers and sat down beside me. "Okay, this one is the test of you and Samantha. In more numbers than words, it states that you are Samantha's biological mother. These numbers here indicate that Tim is her biological father." He looked over at me.

A smile brightened my face. "She's really my daughter, our daughter?" Tears welded in my eyes, not of sadness but of joy and happiness. The same happiness that Tim had always wanted me to find.

"Yes, she's your daughter, Tim's daughter," he smiled with a nod. He looked down and shuffled the paper under the other one. "This test is the DNA of Martha Berkley, also known as Kathy Sonnets. She is not the mother, as you know, but she's the little girl's Aunt."

Kathy Sonnets was the surrogate mother. That's why Tim was uncertain about the name when he came across it. He had heard it before, I thought. "So, she's Tim's sister? He was right about her," I stated.

"Well, not exactly," Brice concluded. "Although, some of the numbers between Tim and Martha/Kathy match, there is no definite relation between them," he said.

I knew I looked flustered, so he continued.

"She's your sister."

"What?" I wasn't sure I'd heard him correctly. "My sister, but I don't have a sister. I don't even have a brother. The test has to be incorrect!"

"No, I'm sorry. I checked her DNA with Tim's and then did one with yours. She's not your full-blooded sister, but your half-sister. One of your parents had a child by someone else, and my presumption is your father. Though, of course, to be certain we'd have to have his DNA checked as well."

"Not possible," I whispered.

"Why? Is he dead?" Brice asked.

I nodded, "He was killed in a car accident when Martha/Kathy was fourteen." I had remembered reading that in Tim's journal. Then it came to me, why would her last name be Sonnets if mine were Stevens? As my brain thought back, the only conclusion would be that I had had my mother's maiden name. She must have changed it back after he left. Although there was no way of asking her, I knew where I could find the truth. I stood and walked to the bookshelf against the wall and pulled out my mother's family tree album. She had made me this book when I started first grade. I flipped the cover open and right inside was written Rose Anne Stevens, my mother's name.

Although, it had come to me just now that I would never know the whole truth about whether Martha/Kathy knew that we were related and that maybe she had contacted Tim knowing this fact, she was dead. As for why Tim never tried to fight for Samantha and get her back to us, is also something I'll never really know the truth about. I believe Martha/Kathy had changed her name to get away from Tim, but even with his expertise and access to records, he was still unable to find our daughter. Our Samantha. Still more questions that will have to go unanswered; something I will have to except.

I walked back to the sofa and sat down next to Brice as if I hadn't moved to get the book, he continued in surprise.

"Oh, I see. Well…" he paused. "I'm sorry about your loss then. Deanna said Martha was killed in prison."

I nodded still in shock. I had a sister, a half sister. From what little I'd known of her, I felt repulsive by the thought. The woman abused my daughter! Her half niece! She was mean and bitter when I went to visit her. Sure, I hadn't known, neither of us did, but still a woman like that would never be a sister to me, half or whole!

"Carla, will you be all right? Should I have Deanna come over to be with you?"

I shook my head, "No, I'm fine, really. Is there anything else on those papers I need to be aware of?"

"No, that's all there is," Brice replied and handed the papers to me.

"Thanks," I said as I took the papers from Brice and watched him stand.

"If you need anything, anything at all, please don't hesitate to ask. We're right next-door, if you need us," Brice stated with a smile. "Carla, I'm so happy for you. Samantha will be the luckiest little girl alive."

"No, I'm the luckiest person to have such a wonderful, smart, and beautiful daughter." I stood and walked him to the door, "Thanks for everything you did, Brice."

"Anything for you, Carla," he replied and walked out the door and down the steps.

Before I closed the door, Samantha spoke, "Is it true? Are you my real mom?" Samantha asked from the doorway of the kitchen.

I shut the door and turned around before one word exited my mouth. No more lies I thought. No more hiding the truth from the people we love the most. No more secrets—period!

"Yes, I'm really your mom and Tim was your dad. He was the one who made it possible to bring you into this world." It was all I could say.

Samantha ran towards me with a huge smile on her face. I opened my arms and scooped her up into the air. We hugged each other tight and twirled around, laughter filling the room around us.

This was what it was supposed to be like. A house filled with love and laughter, but mostly, happiness. I missed Tim more than anything, but knew deep inside that he was here with me, with both of us. Especially when I looked at Samantha; things I hadn't noticed before, I saw now. His eyes and his smile. She had his loving heart, his will to make everything around him shine!

In the end, I finally had a child, not a baby, but it no longer mattered to me whether it was a baby or a child. Samantha was mine, would always be mine, until the end of time.

As I twirled her around, the light in the kitchen got dim then bright. I stopped and moved forward to get a better look, while still holding Samantha in my arms. My mouth fell open as the shadows of two people came into view. The old lady I'd seen twice in the past two months and Tim holding Mya in his arms were standing in my kitchen. They smiled at me. I placed Samantha down and walked towards them.

"My sweet child, you've finally found your happiness," my mother said. "I miss you so much, my sweet girl."

I nodded, tears flowing down my face. This woman was my mom, but how can they be here? I never thought once that ghosts were real; that people could appear from the dead, but they were here right in front of me; I was sure of it.

Tim reached his hand out as if to brush the tears away. "I will always love you, Carla," he whispered and then looked down at Samantha. "My beautiful girl, I will always be watching over you from above. Both of you." Tim blew us a kiss and with a squeeze of their hands, they both disappeared from the room as if they never existed.

I wasn't going to sit and question what I had just seen; I knew what I saw; and I believe Samantha saw it as well.

I looked down at her; she smiled her toothless grin back at me. "Who was the woman with my daddy?" she asked.

"That was your grandma. She's in heaven with your daddy and Mya, your sister. They'll all be watching over us," I replied.

I lifted her up and wrapped my arms around my daughter, spinning her around, and filling the empty room with laughter—once more.

All the happiness in the world was commingling in this room at this moment. Nothing could ever compare to the love a mother has for her child. Everything that I had ever wanted had finally, in some way, come true.

Acknowledgements

I must start by giving many thanks and appreciation to my editor Deborah Bowman Stevens. She takes my writing and turns it into a priceless gem. I don't know what I'd do without her, helping me every step of the way.

I'd also like to give my thanks to Cynthia Maraczi who has given me the medical procedures about NICU and babies being born at six-months, instead of nine. The battle the newborn has to face along with their loving parents who are staying patient as they endure all that may come before they are able to go home and be cared for by their parents. And to the doctor's and nurse's who work day in and day out to help the baby/babies to survive.

It's hard to imagine without going through it myself, which I have not. My heart goes out to the mothers and fathers of the children born into this world excessively early. May God be with you and your family.

Many thanks to my family who for some unknown reason believe in me and stand by me through my writing.

About the Author

Donna M. Zadunajsky started out writing children's books before she accomplished and published her first novel, *Broken Promises*, in June 2012. She then has written several more novels and her first novella, *HELP ME!* which is a subject about suicide and bullying.

She is currently working on an adult novel series and a Young Adult series about self-harm and suicide topics.

Novels: by Donna M. Zadunajsky

Broken Promises
Not Forgotten
Family Secrets "Secrets and Second Chances", Book 1

Children's Books By Donna M. Zadunajsky

Tayla's Best Day Ever!
Tayla's Best Friend
Tayla's New Friend
Tayla Goes to Grammie's House
Tayla Takes a Trip
Tayla's Day at the Beach
Tayla's First Day of School

Novellas By Donna M. Zadunajsky

HELP ME!